The Weapon Makers

A. E. van Vogt

NEW ENGLISH LIBRARY
TIMES MIRROR

Originally published in the United States of America by Greenberg Publications, Inc.
© by A. E. van Vogt 1947
© by Street & Smith Publications, Inc. 1952
Published in Great Britain by Weidenfeld & Nicolson in 1954

*

FIRST NEL EDITION FEBRUARY 1970

*

NEL Books are published by
New English Library Limited from Barnard's Inn, Holborn, London E.C.1.
Made and printed in Great Britain by Hunt Barnard & Co. Ltd., Aylesbury, Bucks.

45000444 9

THE WEAPON MAKERS

1

HEDROCK ALMOST FORGOT THE SPY RAY. IT CONTINUED TO glow, the picture on the screen showing the Imperial conference room as clearly as ever. There were still men bowing low over the hand of the cold-faced young woman who sat on the throne chair, and the sound of their voices came distinctly. Everything was as it should be.

For Hedrock, however, all interest in that palatial room, that courtly scene, had faded. The icy words of the young woman spun around and around in his mind, though minutes had now passed since she had spoken them.

"—Under the circumstances," she had said, "we cannot afford to take further risks with this Weapon Shop turncoat. What has happened is too important. Accordingly, General Grall, you will, as a purely precautionary measure, arrest Captain Hedrock an hour after lunch and hang him. The time sequence is important, as he will, as usual, sit at my table during lunch, and also because I wish to be present at the execution."

"Very well, Your Majesty—"

Hedrock paced back and forth in front of his viewing machine. Finally, he stared again at the screen, which, in its present materialized form, occupied an entire corner of the apartment. He saw, with a somber awareness, that the young woman was still in the conference room, alone now. She sat, a faint smile on her long face. The smile faded as she touched an instrument on her chair and began to dictate in a clear, bell-like voice.

For a moment, Hedrock allowed the meaning of the routine palace matters she was discussing to penetrate his mind; then he withdrew his attention. There was a purpose in his mind, a hardening determination not to accept the failure that was here. Very carefully, he began to adjust his machine. The scene showing the young empress faded. The viewing plate flickered with formless light, finally caught the face of a man, and steadied. Hedrock said, "Calling the High Council of the Weapon Makers."

"It will take a minute," said the man on the screen, gravely, "to bring the various councilors to their locals."

Hedrock nodded stiffly. He was suddenly nervous. His voice

had been steady enough, but he had the feeling that it would deteriorate into a quaver. He stood very still, consciously relaxing the tension. When he looked again at the screen, a dozen faces had replaced the one; enough members for a quorum. He began at once an account of the sentence of death that had been pronounced on him. He finished, finally: "There is no doubt that something important is happening. Time and again during the last two weeks, when an Imperial conference has been called, I have found myself headed off into tedious conversations with superior officers, prevented from returning to my rooms. To my mind, however, the significant factor of the hanging order is the time element involved. Note that I am not to be arrested until an hour after lunch, that is, about three hours from now. And then, too, I was allowed to return to my apartment in time to hear the sentence pronounced. If they know the Weapon Shops, they must realize that, given three hours warning, I have ample time to escape."

"Are you suggesting," said Councilor Peter Cadron sharply, "that you are going to remain?"

The cold, stiff feeling came back to Hedrock. When he spoke again, his voice shook the faintest bit though the words themselves were precise and, in their essence, confident: "You will remember, Mr. Cadron, that we have analysed the Empress' character. The abnormal sociotechnical pressures of the age have made her as restless and as adventure-minded as are her nineteen billion subjects. She wants change, excitement, new experiences. But above everything else she is the Imperial power, representative of the conservative, anti-change forces. The result is a constant tug of mind, a dangerous state of unbalance, which makes her the most difficult enemy the Weapon Shops have had in many centuries."

"The hanging, no doubt," said another man coldly, "will supply a fillip to her jaded nerves. For the few moments that you jerk and bounce in the noose, her life will seem less drab."

"What I had in mind," said Hedrock steadily, "was that one of our No-men might resolve the various factors and advise on the practicability of my remaining."

"We will consult Edward Gonish," said Peter Cadron. "Now please have patience while we discuss this matter privately."

They withdrew, but not visually, for their faces remained on the viewer, and though Hedrock could see their lips move, no voice came through. The conversation went on for a very long time, and there was a seemingly endless period when something was being explained to somebody not on the screen. The time grew so long that Hedrock stood finally with teeth clamped tight, and clenched hands. He sighed with relief as the silence ended, and Peter Cadron said:

8

THE WEAPON MAKERS

"We must regretfully report that the No-man, Edward Gonish, considers that there are not sufficient known factors for him to offer an intuition. This leaves us with only logic, and so we wish to ask one question: At what time will your present chances of escaping from the palace begin to deteriorate sharply? Can you possibly stay for lunch?"

Hedrock held himself steady, letting the shock of the report of the No-man's verdict drain out of him. He hadn't realized how much he was depending on that superbly trained intuitive genius to decide on *his* life or death. In an instant, the situation had become uncertain and dangerous beyond his previous conception. He said at last, "No, if I stay to lunch I'm committed. The Empress likes to play cat and mouse, and she will definitely inform me of the sentence during the meal. I have a plan, dependent on her emotional reactions and based on the fact that she will consider it necessary to justify herself."

He paused, frowning at the screen. "What were the conclusions of your discussion? I need every possible assistance."

It was Councilor Kendlon, a thick-faced man who had hitherto not spoken, who said, "As you know, Hedrock, you are in the palace for two purposes, one being to protect the Weapon Shops from a surprise attack during what we have all agreed is a dangerous time for our civilization. Your other purpose is, of course, your own pet scheme of establishing a liaison between the Weapon Shops and the Imperial government. You are a spy, therefore, only in a minor sense. Any lesser information you may gain is yours alone. We do not want it. But think back in your mind: Have you heard anything – *anything* – that might provide a foundation for your theory that something tremendous is being planned?

Hedrock shook his head slowly. Quite suddenly, he felt no emotion. He had a sense of being physically detached. He spoke finally as out of a remote, cold region, precisely, evenly, conclusively, "I can see, sirs, that you have come to no decision, yet you cannot deny that you are reluctant to have my connection here broken. And there is no doubt of your anxiety to learn what the Empress is concealing. Finally, there is, as you say, my pet scheme. Accordingly, I have decided to remain."

They were not so quick as that to agree. The strange, restless character of the empress made it possible that the slightest wrong word on his part would be fatal. Details – details – they discussed them with a painstaking thoroughness. There was the fact that he was the first apparent traitor to the Weapon Shops in history, one who nevertheless refused to give any information to the curious ruler. His striking appearance, mental brilliance and strong personality had already fascinated her, and should continue to do so. Therefore, except for the fact that she was engaged in something secret and important, the threat of hanging was a test, product of suspicion. But be careful. If necessary, give her secret Weapon Shop information of a general nature, to titillate her appetite for more and—

At that point the door buzzer broke off the conversation. With a start, Hedrock flicked off the controls, and shut off the power. Then, acutely conscious that he had allowed himself to become jumpy, he deliberately removed the plain gold pin from his tie, and bent down over the table. The ring lay there, a small, bright design, its ornamental head an exact duplicate of the spy-ray machine, the image of which was built up into solid form by the atomic forces manufactured by the perfect power plant inside the ring. It would be quicker to release the tiny, automatic lever that was attached to the ring for that very purpose, but his own nervous condition was more important.

It was as delicate a task as threading a needle. Three times his hand trembled the slightest bit and missed the almost invisible depression that had to be contacted. The fourth time he got it. The spy-ray machine winked out like a smashed light, except that there was no debris, nothing but empty air. Where it had stood on the corner table was only the blanket he had used to protect the table top from scratches. Hedrock whisked the blanket back to the bedroom, and then stood for a moment with the ring in his palm, undecided. He put it finally in a metal box with three other rings, and set the controls of the box to dissolve the rings if there were any tampering. Only the ring gun remained encircled on his finger when at last he walked coolly to answer the insistent buzzer.

Hedrock recognized the tall man who stood in the corridor as one of the Empress' orderlies. The fellow nodded recognition, and said, "Captain, Her Majesty asks me to inform you that lunch is being served, and will you please come at once."

For a moment, Hedrock had the distinct impression that he was the object of a practical joke, and that Imperial Innelda was already playing her little thrill game. It couldn't be lunch time so soon. He glanced at his wrist watch. The little dial showed twelve thirty-five. An hour had passed since he had heard the sentence of death from the Empress' firm, finely shaped mouth.

Actually, the question of whether or not he remained till lunch had not been his to decide. The event had rushed upon him even as he was telling the council that it was an hour away. The reality of his position became clear as he walked along past scores of soldiers who stood in every corridor on his way to the royal dining hall; and that reality was that he

10

was staying. It was so final that Hedrock stopped on the threshold of the great room, stood for a moment, smiling sardonically, and was himself.

Quietly, still smiling faintly, he made his way among the tables of noisy courtiers, and sank into his place five chairs down from the Empress at the head table.

2

THE COCKTAIL AND SOUP COURSES WERE ALREADY PAST. Hedrock sat, more pensive now that he was not physically on the move, waiting for whatever was next. He studied the men around the table, the young, strong, arrogant, intelligent thirty-year-olds who made up the personal following of her Imperial Majesty.

He felt a pang of regret at the thought that it must now end. He had enjoyed his six months among this brilliant gathering. It had been exciting again to watch young people tasting the fruits of stupendous power, an untamed enjoyment of joy that was reminiscent of his own distant past. Hedrock smiled wryly. There was a quality about his immortality that he had not allowed for, a developing disregard of risks until the crisis was upon him, a pre-danger casualness about the danger. He had known, of course, that he would sooner or later involve himself beyond even his secret powers. Now as in the past, only his over-all purpose, as distinct from the purposes that people thought he had, was important.

The Empress' voice rose for the first time above the clamor of conversation and cut off his reverie. "You seem very thoughtful, Captain Hedrock."

Hedrock turned his head slowly to face her. He had been wanting to give her more than the cursory glance he had allowed himself so far. But he had been aware of her green eyes watching him from the moment he had seated himself. Hers was a striking, almost a noble countenance. She had the high-cheeked, firm-chinned facial structure of the famous Isher family; and there was no doubt at all that here was only the latest, not the last member of a star human line. Willful passions and power unlimited had twisted her handsome face. But already it was apparent that the erratic, brilliant Innelda, like all the remarkable men and women who were her ancestors, would carry on through corruption and intrigue, in spite

11

of character defects, and that the extraordinary Isher family would survive another generation.

The important thing now, Hedrock thought with a sharpening alertness, was to bring her out into the open under the most advantageous – for him – circumstances. He said, "I was thinking, Innelda, of your grandmother seven times removed, the lovely Ganeel, the golden-haired Empress. Except for your brown hair, you're very like her as she was in her younger days."

The green eyes looked puzzled. The Empress pursed her lips, and then parted them as if to say something. Before she could speak, Hedrock went on, "The Weapon Shops have an entire pictorial of her life. What I was thinking of was the rather sad idea that some day you, too, would be but a pictorial record in some dusty Information Center."

It struck deep. He had known that this young woman could not bear the thought of old age or death in connection with herself. Anger brought a gleam to her eyes, and produced as it always had in the past what she was really thinking.

"You at least," she snapped in a brittle, yet ringing voice, "will not live to see any pictorial of my life. You may be interested to know, my dear captain, that your spy work here has been found out, and you are to be hanged this afternoon."

The words shocked him. It was one thing to theorize in advance that here was nothing but a cunning, murderous test, a determined attempt to draw him out—and quite another to sit here beside this woman, who could be so cruel and merciless and yet whose every whim was law, and hear her pronounce his death sentence. Against such a flesh and blood tyrant, all logic was weak, all theory unreal and fantastic.

Abruptly, it was difficult to understand the reasoning that had made him place himself in such a predicament. He could so easily have waited another generation, or two, or more, for a woman to turn up again in the Isher line. It was true, of course, that this was the logical point, both biologically and historically. He ended the thought and fought off the black mood. He forced himself, then, to relax and to smile. After all, he had drawn that answer out of her, clearly before she really wanted to announce the sentence. In a grisly sort of way, it was a psychological victory. A few more victories like that, however, and he'd be all set for a nervous breakdown.

There was still conversation going on in the great dining room, but not at the royal table. That brought Hedrock back to full awareness of his environment. Some of the young men were sitting staring at the Empress. Others looked at Hedrock, then at the Empress, then at Hedrock again. All were transparently puzzled. They seemed uncertain as to whether it was

12

a bad joke or one of the damnable real-life dramas that the Empress precipitated from time to time, seemingly for the sole purpose of ruining everybody's digestion. The important thing, Hedrock thought tightly, was that the situation now had the full attention of the men whom he expected to save his life.

It was the Empress who broke the silence. She said softly, tauntingly, "A penny for your *latest* thoughts, Captain."

She couldn't have put it better. Hedrock suppressed a savage smile, and said, "My earlier statement still holds. You're very like the lovely, temperamental, explosive Ganeel. The main difference is that she never slept with a live snake when she was sixteen."

"What's this?" said a courtier. "Innelda sleeping with snakes? Is this intended symbolically or literally? Why look, she's blushing."

It was so. Hedrock's cool gaze studied the Empress' scarlet-cheeked confusion with amazed curiosity. He had not expected to obtain so violent a response. In a moment, of course, there would be a flood of bad temper. It wouldn't disturb most of the bold young men, who had, each in his own way, found that middle path between yes-man and individual that the young woman demanded of all her personal followers.

"Come, come, Hedrock," said the mustachioed Prince del Curtin, "you're not going to keep this splendid tidbit to yourself. I suppose this also is derived from the pictorial files of the Weapon Shops."

Hedrock was silent. His smile of acknowledgment seemed to be directed at the prince-cousin of the Empress, but actually he scarcely saw the man. His gaze and attention were concentrated on the only person in the room who mattered. The Empress Isher sat, the flush on her face slowly yielding to anger. She climbed to her feet, a dangerous glint in her eyes, but her voice had in it only a fraction of the fury that he had hoped for. She said grimly: "It was very clever of you, Captain Hedrock, to twist the conversation the way you did. But I assure you it won't do you the slightest good. You're swift response merely confirms that you were aware in advance of my intention. You're a spy, and we're taking no more chances with you."

"Oh, come now, Innelda," said a man. "You're not going to pull a miserable stunt like that."

"You watch out, mister," the woman flared, "or you'll join him on the scaffold."

The men at the table exchanged significant glances. Some of them shook their heads disapprovingly, and then all of them fell to talking among themselves, ignoring the Empress.

Hedrock waited. This was what he had been working for,

but now that it was here, it seemed inadequate. In the past, ostracism by the men whose companionship she valued had had a great emotional effect on the ruler. Twice since his arrival he had seen it influence her decisively. But not this time. The realization penetrated to Hedrock with finality as he watched the woman sink back into her chair, and sit there, her long, handsome face twisted satirically. Her smile faded. She said gravely: "I'm sorry, gentlemen, that you feel as you do. I regret any outburst which would seem to indicate that my decision against Captain Hedrock was a personal one. But I have been greatly upset by my discovery that he is a spy."

It was impressive. It had a convincing ring to it, and the men's private conversations, which had died while she was speaking, did not resume. Hedrock leaned back in his chair, his sense of defeat stronger with each passing second. Quite clearly, whatever was behind the execution was too big, too important, for mere cleverness to overbalance.

Drastic, dangerous, deadly action was in order.

For a while, then, he was intent on his own thoughts. The long table with its satin-smooth white linen covering, its golden dishes, its two dozen fine-looking young men, yielded before that intensity, became a background to his ever grimmer purpose. He needed words that would change the whole design of the situation, plus action that would clinch it. He grew aware that Prince del Curtin had been speaking for some moments:

" — You can't just make a statement that a man is a spy, and expect us to believe it. We know you're the biggest and best liar this side of creation when it suits you. If I'd suspected this was coming up, I'd have attended the cabinet meeting this morning. How about a little fact?"

Hedrock felt impatient. The men had already accepted the sentence, though they didn't seem to realise it. The quicker they were cut out of the conversation the better. But careful now. Wait until the Empress had committed herself, regardless of how well she did it. She was, he saw, sitting stiffly, her expression grave, unsmiling. She said quietly: "I'm afraid I shall have to ask you all to trust me. A very serious situation has arisen; it was the sole subject of our council meeting today, and I assure you the decision to execute Captain Hedrock was unanimous, and I am personally distressed by the necessity."

Hedrock said, "I really thought better of your intelligence than this, Innelda. Are you planning another of your futile forays against the Weapon Shops, and think that I might find out about it and report it to the Weapon Shop council?"

Her green eyes blazed at him. Her voice was like chipped steel as she snapped, "I shall say nothing that might give you a

14

clue. I don't know just what kind of a communications system you have with your superiors, but I know that one exists. My physicists have frequently registered on their instruments powerful wave lengths of extremely high range."

"Originating in my room?" asked Hedrock softly.

She stared at him, her lips drawn into an angry frown. She said reluctantly, "You would never have dared come here if you had had to be as obvious as that. I will inform you, sir, that I am not interested in continuing this conversation."

"Though you do not realize it," said Hedrock in his steadiest tone, "I have said all that was necessary to prove my innocence when I disclosed to you that I knew that, at the age of sixteen, you slept one night with a live snake."

"Ah!" said the Empress. Her body shook with triumph. "Now the confession begins. So you expected to have to put up a defense, and you prepared that little speech."

Hedrock shrugged. "I knew something was being prepared for me. My apartment has been searched every day for a week. I've been subjected to the most boring sustained monologues by the prize dunderheads in the Army office. Wouldn't I be a simpleton if I hadn't thought of every angle?"

"What I don't understand," chimed in a young man, "is the snake business. Why do you think your knowledge of that proves you not guilty? That's too deep for me."

"Don't be such an ass, Maddern," said Prince del Curtin. "It simply means that the Weapon Shops knew intimate details of Innelda's palace life long before Captain Hedrock ever came. It shows the existence of a spy system more dangerous than anything we ever suspected, and the real charge against Captain Hedrock is that he has been remiss in not telling us that such a system existed."

Hedrock was thinking: Not yet, not yet. Somewhere along here the crisis would come suddenly, and then his action must be swift, perfectly timed, decisive. Aloud, he said coolly, "Why should you worry? Three thousand years have proven that the Weapon Shops have no intention of overthrowing the Imperial government. I know for a fact that the spy ray is used with great discretion, and has never been employed at night except on the occasion that Her Majesty had the snake smuggled in from the palace zoo. Curiosity made the two women scientists in charge of the machine on that occasion continue their watch. The story was, of course, too good to keep in a file. And you may be interested, Your Majesty, to know that two psychological articles were written about it, one by our greatest living No-man, Edward Gonish."

From the corners of his eyes Hedrock saw that the slim, lithe body of the woman was leaning forward, her lips were

15

slightly parted, her eyes wide with an intense interest. Her whole being seemed to move according to his words. "What," she half whispered, "did he say about me?"

With a shock, Hedrock recognized his moment. Now, he thought, *now!*

He was trembling. But he couldn't help his physical condition, nor did he care. A man threatened with death was expected to show agitation, or else he was considered unhuman, cold—and received no sympathy. His voice rose against the pattern of babble from distant tables, a little wildly and passionately. But that, too, was good, for a woman was staring at him with wide eyes, a woman who was half child, half genius, and who hungered with all her intense emotional nature for the strange and exotic. She sat with shining eyes, as Hedrock said:

"You must be mad, all of you, or you would not constantly underestimate the Weapon Shops and their lineally-developed science. What a petty idea it is that I have come here as a spy, that I am curious about some simple little government secret. I am here for one purpose only, and Her Majesty is perfectly aware of what it is. If she kills me she is deliberately destroying her better, greater self; and if I know anything about the Isher line in the final issue they draw back from suicide."

The Empress was straightening, frowning. "The presumption of your purpose," she snapped, "is only equalled by your cleverness."

Hedrock paid no attention to the interruption. He refused to give up the initiative. He rushed on, "It is apparent that you have all forgotten your history, or are blinding yourself to the reality. The Weapon Shops were founded several thousand years ago by a man who decided that the incessant struggle for power of different groups was insane, and that civil and other wars must stop forever. It was a time when the world had just emerged from a war in which more than a billion people had died, and he found thousands of individuals who agreed to follow him to the death. His idea was nothing less than that whatever government was in power should not be overthrown. But that an organization should be set up which would have one principal purpose: to ensure that no government ever again obtained complete power over its people.

"A man who felt himself wronged should be able to go somewhere to buy a defensive gun. What made this possible was the invention of an electronic and atomic system of control which made it possible to build indestructible weapon shops, and to manufacture weapons that could only be used for defense. That last ended all possibility of Weapon Shop

16

guns being used by gangsters and criminals, and morally justified placing dangerous instruments in the hands of anyone
who needed protection.

"At first people thought that the Shops were a sort of underground anti-government organization that would itself protect
them from harm. But gradually they realized that the Shops
did not interfere in Isher life. It was up to each individual or
group of individuals to save their own lives. The idea was that
the individual would learn to stand up for himself, and that in
the long run the forces which would normally try to enslave
him would be restrained by the knowledge that a man or a
group could be pressed only so far. And so a great balance
was struck between those who govern and those who are governed.

"It turned out that a further step was necessary, not as a
protection against the government, but against rapacious private enterprise. Civilization became so intricate that the average person could not protect himself against the cunning
devices of those who competed for his money. Accordingly, a
system of Weapon Shop courts was set up, to which people
could turn when they felt themselves aggrieved in this
fashion."

Out of the corner of his eye, Hedrock saw that the Empress
was becoming restive. She was not a Weapon Shop admirer,
and since his purpose was to impress with the absurdity of her
suspicions, and not to change her basic attitude, he came to
his point:

"What is not clearly realized by the government forces is
that the Weapon Shops are, because of their scientific
achievements, more powerful than the government itself. They
understand of course that if they should be foolish enough
to overthrow the Empress they would not necessarily have the
support of the population, and that in fact they would upset
the stability which their presence has made possible. *Nevertheless, the superiority is a fact.* For that reason alone, the
Empress' accusation against me is meaningless, and must have
some other motivation than the one she has stated."

Hedrock had too sharp a sense of dramatic values to pause
there. His main point was made, but the reality was so harsh
that he instantly needed a distraction, something on a different
level entirely; and which, yet, would appear to be part of the
whole. He rushed on: "To give you some idea of the great
scientific attainments of the Weapon Shops, I can tell you that
they have an instrument which can predict the moment of
death of any person. Before I came to the palace six months
ago, for my own amusement I secured readings as to the death
moments of almost every person at this table and of the mem-

bers of the Imperial Council."

He had them now. He could see it in the strained faces that looked at him with a feverish fascination. But still he could not afford to lose control of the conversation. With an effort, he forced himself to bow at the white-faced ruler. Then hastily he said, "I am happy to announce, Your Majesty, that you have a long and increasingly honorable life ahead of you. Unfortunately—" His voice took on a darker tone, as he raced on: "Unfortunately, there is a gentleman present who is destined to die—within minutes."

He did not wait to see the effect of that, but turned in his chair, a tigerishly swift movement. For there was no time to waste. Any instant his bluff might be called; and his show would end in a ludicrous failure. His voice bawled across the space that separated him from a table where sat a dozen men in uniform:

"General Grall!"

"Eh!" The officer who was to carry out the hanging order whipped around. He looked startled when he saw who it was.

It struck Hedrock that his bellow had brought complete silence to the room. People at every table had stopped eating, stopped their private conversations, and were watching the royal table, and him. Conscious of his greater audience, Hedrock pushed his voice forward in his mouth, tightened his diaphragm, and brought forth the ringing question, "General Grall, if you were to die this minute, what would be the cause?"

The heavy-faced man two tables away stood up slowly. "I'm in perfect health," he growled. "What the devil are you talking about?"

"Nothing wrong with your heart?" Hedrock urged.

"Not a thing."

Hedrock thrust his chair back and climbed to his feet. He couldn't afford errors due to awkward positions. With a jerk, he raised his arm and pointed at the general with his finger, rudely.

"You're General Lister Grall, are you not?"

"That's right. And now, Captain Hedrock, I resent most violently this—"

Hedrock cut him off, "General, I regret to announce that, according to the records of the Weapon Shops, you are due to die at exactly one fifteen o'clock *today* from heart failure. That's this minute, this—second."

There was no stopping now. With a single, synchronized motion, Hedrock bent his finger, shaped his hand to receive the gun materialized on an invisible plane by the gun ring on his finger.

It was no ordinary, retail-type gun, that unseen, wizard's product, but a special Unlimited never sold across counters,

18

never displayed, never used except in extreme crises. It fired instantly on a vibration plane beyond human vision; and, as the general's heart muscles were caught by the paralysing force, Hedrock unclenched his hand. The invisible gun dematerialized.

In the pandemonium that followed, Hedrock walked to the throne chair at the head of the royal table and bent over the Empress. He could not suppress a tingle of admiration, for she was completely, abnormally calm. Emotional, erotic woman she might be, but in actual moments of excitement, during the hour of vital decision, all the great, basic stability that was her Isher inheritance came to the fore. It was that quality of utter sanity in her that he had appealed to; and here it was, like a precious jewel, shining at him from the quiet viridescence of her eyes. She said finally: "I suppose you realize you have, by implication, confessed everything by your killing of General Grall."

He knew better than to deny anything to the supernal being she had for that sustained moment become. He said, "I was advised of the sentence of death, and by whom it was to be carried out."

"Then you admit it?"

"I'll admit anything you wish so long as you understand that I have your best interests at heart."

She looked incredulous. "A Weapon Shop man, whose organization fights me at every turn, talking about my interests?"

"I am not, never have been, never will be, a Weapon Shop man." Hedrock spoke deliberately.

A startled look came into her face, then, "I almost believe that. There's something strange, and alien, about you, something I must discover—"

"Some day, I'll tell you. I promise."

"You seem very sure that I shall not have somebody else hang you."

"As I said before, the Ishers do not commit suicide."

"Now you're on your old theme, your impossible ambition. But never mind that. I'm going to let you live, but for the time being you must leave the palace. You can't convince me that an all-purpose spy ray exists."

"Can't I?"

"You may have had such a machine prying into the palace when I was sixteen, but since then the whole palace has been fitted with defense screens. Those can be pierced only by a two-way communication machine. In other words, there must be a machine inside as well as out."

"You're very clever."

19

"As for the pretense," the Empress went on, "that the Weapon Shops can see into the future, let me inform you that we know as much about time travel, and its impossible limitations, as the Weapon Shops. The see-saw principle involved is only too clearly recognized, with all its ever-fatal end results. But again, never mind that. I want you to leave for two months. I may call you back before then, but it all depends. Meantime, you may transmit this message to the Weapon Shop council: What I am doing is not in the faintest degree harmful to the Weapon Shops. I swear that on my honor."

For a long moment, Hedrock gazed at her steadily. He said at last, softly, "I am going to make a very profound statement. I haven't the faintest idea of what you are doing, or going to do, but in your adult life I have noticed one thing. In all your major political and economic moves, you are actuated by conservative impulses. Don't do it. Change is coming. Let it come. Don't fight it, but lead it, direct it. Add new laurels of prestige to the famous name of Isher."

"Thank you for your advice," she said coldly.

Hedrock bowed, and said, "I shall expect to hear from you in two months. Goodbye."

The hum of renewed conversation was mounting behind him as he reached the series of ornate doors on the far side of the room. He passed through, and then, out of sight, quickened his pace. He reached the elevators, stepped into one hurriedly, and pressed the express button for the roof. It was a long trip, and his nerves grew jumpy. Any minute, any *second*, that mood of the Empress could wear off.

The elevator stopped, the door opened. He was stepping out before he noticed the body of men. They came forward at the double march and instantly hemmed him in. They were in plain clothes, but there was no mistaking that here were police.

The next instant one of the men said, "Captain Hedrock, you are under arrest."

3

AS HE STOOD THERE ON THE PALACE ROOF FACING THAT score of men, his mind, adjusted to victory, could not accept the threatening defeat. Here were enough men to handle any resistance he might attempt. But that did not slow his purpose.

20

The Empress *must* have known when she gave the order to intercept him that he could only draw the worst conclusions, and fight with every power that he could muster. The time for subtlety, injured innocence and cleverness was past. His deep baritone clashed across the silence:

"What do you want?"

There were great moments in the history of the world when that bellow of his had produced a startled lull in the will to action of better men than any that stood here before him. It had no such effect now.

Hedrock felt astounded. His muscles, dynamically ready for the run that was to take him through the ranks of the men while they stood paralysed, tensed. The large carplane which had seemed so near a moment before, only twenty-five feet, tantalized him now. His purpose, to reach it, collapsed into an awareness of his desperate situation. One man with one gun against twenty guns! True, his was an Unlimited, and like all Weapon Shop guns projected a defensive half circle around its owner, sufficient to counteract the fire of eight ordinary weapons, but he had never underestimated the capacity of a blaster.

His hard, mental assessment of his position ended as the huskily built young man who had pronounced him under arrest stepped forward from the group and said crisply, "Now, don't do anything rash, Mr. Weapon Shop Jones. You'd better come quietly."

"Jones!" said Hedrock. Shock made the word quiet, almost gentle. Shock and relief. For a moment, the gap between his first assumption and the reality seemed too great to bridge without some superhuman effort of will. The next second he had caught hold of himself and the tension was over. His gaze flashed with lightning appraisal toward the uniformed palace guards who were standing on the fringe of the group of plain-clothes men, interested spectators rather than participants. And he sighed under his breath as their faces remained blank of suspicion. He said, "I'll go quietly."

The plain-clothes men crowded around him, and herded him into the carplane. The machine took off with a lurch, so swiftly was it maneuvered into the air. Breathless, Hedrock sank into the seat beside the man who had given him the Weapon Shop password for the day. He found his voice after a minute.

"Very bravely done," he said warmly. "Very bold and efficient, I may say, though, you gave me a shock."

He laughed at the recollection, and was about to go on when the odd fact struck him that his hearer had not smiled in sympathetic response. His nerves, still keyed to unnatural sensitivity, examined that small, jarring fact. He said slowly, "You don't mind if I ask your name?"

"Peldy," the man said curtly.

"Who thought of the idea of sending you?"

"Councilor Peter Cadron."

Hedrock nodded. "I see. He thought if I had to fight my way to the roof, I'd be needing help by the time I got there.'

"I have no doubt," said Peldy, "that that is part of the explanation."

He was cold, this young man. The chill of his personality startled Hedrock. He stared gloomily down through the transparent floor at the unreeling scene below. The plane, conforming to speed regulations, was slowly heading deeper into the city. The strain of his transcendental purpose, which required that he keep from all men the knowledge that he was immortal, was briefly hard to bear. Hedrock roused himself finally and said, "Where are you taking me?"

"To the hotel."

Hedrock considered that. The Hotel Royal Ganeel was the city headquarters of the Weapon Makers. To be taken there indicated that something serious had happened.

The Hotel Royal Ganeel was about two hundred years old. It had cost, if he remembered correctly, seven hundred and fifty billion credits. Its massive base spread over four city blocks. From this beginning, it went up in pyramidic tiers, steamlined according to the waterfall architecture of its age, leveling off at twelve hundred feet into a roof garden eight hundred feet long by eight hundred feet wide, the hard squareness of which was skilfully alleviated by illusion and design. He had built it in memory of a remarkable woman who was also an Isher empress, and in every room he had installed a device which, properly activated, provided a vibratory means of escape.

The activating instrument, unfortunately, was one of the three rings he had left behind him in the palace. Hedrock grimaced in vexation as he headed with the others from the plane to the nearest elevator. He had spent careful moments deciding not to wear more than the ring gun lest suspicion fall upon those remarkable secret machines of the Weapon Shops. There were other rings in secret panels scattered through the hotel, but it was doubtful if a man with twenty guards escorting him to the great section of the building occupied by the Imperial City headquarters of the Weapon Makers would have any time for side trips.

His reverie ended as the elevator stopped. The men crowded him out on to a broad corridor before a door on which glowing letters spelled out:

The sign, Hedrock knew, was only half false. The gigantic mining trust was a genuine firm, doing a vast metal and manufacturing business. It was also an unsuspected subsidiary of the Weapon Shops, which was aside from the main point except, as in the present instance, where its various offices served as fronts behind which facets of the Weapon Shop world glittered in uninterrupted, unhindered activity.

As Hedrock walked into the great front offices, a tall, fine-looking, middle-aged man was emerging from an opaque door fifty feet away. Recognition was almost simultaneous. The man hesitated the faintest bit, then came forward with a friendly smile.

"Well, Mr. Hedrock," he said, "how's the Empress?"

Hedrock's smile was stiff. The great No-man's hesitation had not been lost on him. He said, "I am happy to say that she is in good health, Mr. Gonish."

Edward Gonish laughed, a rich-toned laughter. "I'm afraid there are thousands of people who are always saddened when they hear that. At the moment, for instance, the council is trying to use my intuitive training to track down the secret of the Empress. I'm studying Pp charts of known and potentially great men. It's miserable data to go on, far less than the ten percent I need. I've only reached the letter M as yet, and I have only come to tentative conclusions. If it's an invention, I would say interstellar travel. But that isn't a full intuitive."

Hedrock frowned. "Interstellar travel! She would be opposed to that—" He stopped; then, in an intense voice: "You've got it! Quick, who's the inventor?"

Gonish laughed again. "Not so fast. I have to go over all the data. I've got my attention on a scientist named Derd Kershaw, if you're interested."

His laughing eyes grew abruptly grave. The No-man stood frowning at Hedrock. He said finally, anxious, "What the devil's up, Hedrock? What have you done?"

The secret police officer, Peldy, stepped forward quickly and said, "Really, Mr. Gonish, the prisoner can't—"

The proud face of the No-man turned coldly on the young man. "That will do," he said. "Step back out of hearing. I wish to talk to Mr. Hedrock alone."

Peldy bowed. "I beg your pardon, sir. I forgot myself."

He backed away, then began to wave his men off. In less than a minute, however, Hedrock was alone with the No-man, the first shock fading in a series of little, mental pain waves. A prisoner! He had known it, of course, in a kind of a way, but

23

he had tried to think of himself as being under suspicion only, and he had hoped that if he pretended not to recognize it, the Weapon Shop leaders might not force the issue into the open.

Gonish was speaking again, swiftly, "The worst part of it is, they refused to listen when I suggested that the whole business be left over for me to investigate in my capacity as No-man. That's bad. Could you give me some idea?"

Hedrock shook his head. "All I know is that two hours ago they were worried that I might be killed by the Empress. They actually sent a rescue force, but it turned out I was, and am, under close arrest."

The tall Gonish stood thoughtful. "If you could only put them off some way," he said. "I don't know enough about the individual psychologies of the councilors or about the case to offer one of my intuitive opinions, but if you can possibly twist the affair into a trial of evidence and counterevidence, that would be a partial victory. They're a pretty highhanded outfit, so don't just knuckle under to their decision as if it were from God."

He walked off, frowning, toward a distant door, and Hedrock grew aware of Peldy striding forward. "This way, sir," the young man said. "The Council will see you immediately."

"Eh?" said Hedrock. The sense of warmth produced by the No-man's friendly intent faded. "You mean, the Council is in the local chamber?"

There was no answer, nor did he really expect one. Stiffly erect, he followed the secret-police officer to the door of the council chamber.

The men sitting at the V-shaped table lifted their eyes and stared at him as he crossed the threshold into the room. The door closed behind him with a faint click as he walked forward toward the table. It seemed strange to be thinking that two years before he had refused to run for a seat on the council. The councilors were of every age, ranging from the brilliant thirty-year-old executive, Ancil Nare, to hoary-headed Bayd Roberts. Not all the faces were familiar to him. Hedrock counted noses, thinking about what the No-man had said: "Make it a trial!" That meant, force them out of their smug rut. He finished his counting, shocked. Thirty! The full council of the Weapon Makers. What could they have found out about him, to bring all of them here? He pictured these leaders at their headquarters far and near, on Mars, Venus, on those moons that rated so exalted a representative—*everywhere* councilors stepping through their local vibratory transmitters, and instantly arriving here.

All for him. Abruptly, that was startling again. And steadying. With shoulders thrown back, fully conscious of his leonine head, and of his unmistakably notable appearance, aware, too, of the generations of men like this who had lived and died, and lived and died, and died, and died, since his own birth—Hedrock broke the silence. "What's the charge?" he asked resonantly. And into those words he put all the subtle, tremendous power of his trained voice, his vast experience in dealing with every conceivable type and group of' human beings.

There was a stirring along the gleaming V-table. Feet shuffled on the dimly glowing dais. Men turned to look at each other questioningly. It was Peter Cadron who finally climbed to his feet. "I have been asked," he said quietly, "to speak for the council. It was I who originated the charge against you." He did not wait for a reply, but turned slowly to face the men at the table. He said gravely, "I am sure that everyone present has suddenly become acutely aware of the personality of Mr. Hedrock. It is interesting to note how exactly this exhibition of hitherto concealed power verifies what we have discovered. I must confess my own amazement at the vivid force of it."

"That goes for me, too," interrupted the heavy-faced Deam Lealy. "Until this minute I thought of Hedrock as a soft-spoken, reserved sort of fellow. Now, suddenly, he's cornered and he flashes fire."

"There's no doubt," said the youthful Ancil Nare, "that we've uncovered something remarkable. We should strive for a thorough explanation."

It was disconcerting. His entire action was being enlarged upon beyond his intent, distorted by an expectation that he was not what he seemed. *"What is the charge?"* Hedrock asked again majestically.

There was silence. Then Peter Cadron said, "You will learn that in due time. But first—Mr. Hedrock, where were you born?"

So they had got *that* far.

He felt no fear. He stood there, a little sad, conscious of amusement that his oldest bogey had at last come home to roost. It was possible that he had grown careless.

He said, "You have my records. I was born in Centralia, Middle Lakeside States."

"You took a long time answering that question," snapped a councilor.

"I was," said Hedrock coolly, "trying to imagine what lay behind the question."

Cadron said, "What was your mother's name?"

Hedrock studied the man's even-featured countenance in the beginning of puzzlement. Surely they didn't expect to confuse him with anything so simple as that. He said, "Delmyra Marlter."

"She had three other children?"

Hedrock nodded. "My two brothers and sister all died before reaching their majority."

"And your father and mother died when?"

"My father eight years ago, my mother six."

Amazingly, that came hard. For a bare moment, it was difficult to employ those intimate terms for two pleasant middle-aged people whom he had never met, but about whom he had forced himself to learn so much. He saw that Cadron was smiling with dark satisfaction at the other councilors.

Cadron said, "You see, gentlemen, what we have here: A man whose people are deceased, who has no living relatives, and who less than ten years ago, after all his family was dead, entered the Weapon Shop organization in the usual manner —and by means of talents considered extraordinary even then, when we didn't know how much of himself he was holding back, quickly rose to a position of great trust. Subsequently he persuaded us to sponsor his present adventure. We agreed to do so because we had become alarmed that the Empress might do us harm unless she was watched more carefully than previously. One of the important factors to consider now is that it is doubtful if, in all our vast organization, with its tens of thousands of able men, a single other person could have been found who was capable of sustaining the interest of the Empress Innelda for six long months."

"And even now," Hedrock interrupted, "has only been temporarily banished from her circle." He finished sardonically, "You have not been interested, but *that* was the result of the turmoil in the palace today. The time involved, if I may add the information, is two months."

Peter Cadron bowed at him politely, then turned back to the silent men at the table. "Bear that in mind while I question Mr. Hedrock about his education." His gray gaze glowed at Hedrock. "Well?" he said.

"My mother," said Hedrock, "had been a university professor. She taught me privately. As you know, that has been common practice among the well-to-do for hundreds of years, the controlling factor being that periodic examinations must be passed. You will find that I handed in my examination certificates with my application."

The dark smile was back on Cadron's face. "A family on paper, an education—on paper; an entire life history verifiable only by documents."

It looked bad. Hedrock did not need to look at the faces of the councilors to realize how bad. Actually, of course, it was

26

unavoidable. There never had been an alternative method. To have trusted to a living person to back up his identity in a crisis would have been suicidal. People, however friendly to you, however much they had been paid, could be made to tell the truth. But no one could ever more than cast suspicion on a properly executed certificate. He refused to believe that they had guessed even near the real truth.

"Look here!" he said, "what are you trying to prove? If I'm not Robert Hedrock, who am I?"

He gained a bleak content from the baffled expression that crept over Cadron's face. "That," the man rapped finally, "is what we are trying to find out. However, one more question. After your parents were married, your mother didn't keep in touch with her university friends, or any former colleagues?"

Hedrock hesitated, staring straight into the councilor's glinting eyes. "It fits in, doesn't it, Mr. Cadron?" he said at last in a tight, hard voice. "But you're right. We lived in apartments. My father's work kept us moving every few months. It is doubtful if you can find anyone who will remember having met them or me. We truly lived a shadow existence."

There was a subtle psychological victory in having spoken the indictment himself but—Hedrock smiled grayly—if ever he had heard a damning build-up of innuendo, here it was. He grew aware that Cadron was speaking.

"—We recognize, Mr. Hedrock, that this is not evidence, nor is that what we are after. The Weapon Shops do not hold trials in any real sense. They pass judgments. And the sole criterion always is, not proof of guilt, but doubt of innocence. If you had attained a less exalted position with the Shops, the punishment would be very simple. You would be given amnesia and released from service. As it is, you know too much about us, and accordingly the penalty must be very severe. You know that, in our position, we *cannot* do otherwise. Fortunately for our peace of mind, we have more than suspicion. Is it possible that you have anything to add to what has already gone?"

"Nothing," said Hedrock.

He stood very still, letting his mind settle around the situation. He had originally, by secret maneuvering, persuaded the Meteor Corporation to take offices near the roof of the Hotel Royal Ganeel because it had seemed to him that their unsuspected Imperial City headquarters would be safer in a building of h'is than anywhere else, For his own protection, however, he had had removed out of their part of the building all those ring activators and vibratory devices which now he needed so desperately. If he hadn't had that forethought, there would now be a ring behind *that* panel.

Peter Cadron was speaking, the charge at long last. It was hard at first for Hedrock to keep his mind on the man's words. Naturally in arriving at their decision, the psychologists made a swift though careful examination of his psychology chart. It was this examination that brought out an extraordinary fact.

Peter Cadron paused. His gaze fixed on Hedrock's face, and for a moment he seemed to be probing in its lineaments for secret information. He finished weightily, "There was a variation between your courage in action and the Pp record of your potential courage. According to the Pp you would never even have considered staying for that dangerous luncheon at the palace."

Cadron stopped, and Hedrock waited for him to finish. The seconds passed, and suddenly he was startled to see that dozens of the men were leaning forward tensely, sharp eyes fixed on him. They were waiting for his reaction. It was all over. This was the charge.

The Pp record technique! Hedrock tried to concentrate his mind on remembering what he had heard about the machine. It was one of the original inventions, many thousands of years old. In the beginning it had been similar to the Imperial Lambeth Mind Control. There had been improvements from time to time, a widening of its scope, the power to assess intelligence, emotional stability, and other things. But it had never worried him, who had a partial ability to control his mind. At the time of the examination he had simply attempted to synchronize his intellectual attributes with the character he had decided would best suit his purpose among the Weapon Makers.

Hedrock shook himself like a stag at bay. Damned if he'd believe they had anything. "So," he said, and his voice sounded harsh in his own ears, "so I'm five percent braver than I ought to be. I don't believe it. Bravery is a matter of circumstances. A coward becomes a lion given the proper incentive."

In spite of himself, his voice was suddenly more forceful. Some of the fire of his convictions, his dark anxieties, thickened and deepened his tone. "You people," he snapped, "do not seem to be alive to what is going on. What is happening is no idle whim of a bored ruler. The Empress is a mature personality in all except minor meanings of the terms, and it must never be forgotten that we are now entering into the fifth period of the House of Isher. At any hour mighty events could erupt from the under-currents of human unrest. Twenty billion minds are active, uneasy, rebellious. New frontiers of science and relations among men are beyond the near horizon, and somewhere out of that chaotic mass will grow the fifth crisis of cosmic proportions in the history of the Isher civilization. Only a new development on a high level could bring the Empress to such sustained, forceful action at this stage of her career. She said that in two months she would call me back, and suggested it might be less. It *will* be less. My impression, and I cannot emphasize it too strongly, is that we shall be lucky to have two days. Two weeks is the outside limit."

He was roused now. He saw that Cadron was trying to speak, but he plunged on, unheeding. His voice filled the room. "The entire available trained strength of the Weapon Shops should be concentrating in Imperial City. Every street should have its observer. The fleet should be mobilized within striking distance of the city. All this should be already in ceaseless operation. But what do I find instead?" He paused, then finished scathingly, "The mighty Weapon Shop council is frittering its time away on some obscure discussion of whether or not a man should have been as brave as he was.

He ended, drably conscious that he had not influenced them. The men sat unsmiling, cold. Peter Cadron broke the silence quietly. "The difference," he said, "is seventy-five percent, not five. That's a lot of bravery, and we shall now discuss it briefly."

Hedrock sighed his recognition of defeat. And felt better. Wryly, he recognized why. Against all reason, there had been hope in him. Now there wasn't. Here was the crisis, product of a scientific force which he had thought under control. And it wasn't. His life now depended on moment to moment developments. He listened intently as Cadron spoke again.

"I assure you, Mr. Hedrock," the man said with quiet sincerity, "we are all distressed by the duty that devolves upon us. But the evidence is relentless. Here is what happened: When the psychologists discovered the variation, two cerebro-geometric configurations were set up on the Pp machine. One used as a base the old record of your mind; the other took into account a *seventy-five percent increase in every function of your mind,* EVERY FUNCTION, I repeat, not only courage. Among other things, this brought your I.Q. to the astounding figure of two hundred seventy eight."

Hedrock said, "You say, *every* function. Including idealism and altruism, I presume?"

He saw that the men were looking at him uneasily. Cadron said, "Mr. Hedrock, a man with that much altruism would regard the Weapon Shops as merely one factor in a greater game. The Weapon Shops cannot be so broad-minded. But let me go on. In both the cerebro-geometric configurations I have mentioned, the complicated configuration of the Empress was mechanically woven into the matrix, and because speed was an essential, the possible influence on the situation of other

29

minds was reduced to a high level Constant, modified by a simple, oscillating Variable—"

In spite of himself, Hedrock found himself becoming absorbed. His conviction that he ought to interrupt as often as was psychologically safe yielded before a gathering fascination in the details of a science that had so greatly outstripped his capacity even for learning about it. Graphs of brain and emotional integers, curious mathematical constructions whose roots delved deep into the obscure impulses of the human mind and body. He listened and watched, intently, as Cadron went on with his damning words:

"The problem, as I have said, was to insure that the rescue party did not arrive at the palace too soon, or too late. It was found that the graph based on your old Pp proved that you would never leave the place alive, unless an Unknown of the third order intervened in your favor. That configuration was instantly abandoned. Science cannot take account of possible miracles. The second projection centralized on the hour of 1:40 P.M., with a concentric error possibility of four minutes. The landing therefore, was effected at 1:35, the false Imperial credentials were accepted within two minutes. At 1:39 you emerged from the elevator. You will agree, I think, that the evidence is conclusive."

It was a nightmare. All these years while he had been living and planning, carefully building up the structure of his hopes, he had actually already committed his fortunes to the Pp machine, possibly the greatest invention ever developed in the field of the human mind. Distractedly, Hedrock realized that one of the councilors, not Cadron, but a little gray-haired man, was saying:

"In view of the fact that this is not a criminal case in an ordinary sense of the term, and particularly because of Mr. Hedrock's past services, I think he is entitled to assurance that we are taking seriously what the Empress is doing. For your information, young man, our staff here has been enlarged fivefold. Perhaps in your personal anxiety at the time, you did not notice that the elevator from the airport went down much farther than usual to reach here. We have taken over seven additional floors of the hotel and our organization *is* in ceaseless operation. Unfortunately, in spite of your stirring appeal, I must agree with Mr. Cadron. The Weapon Shops, being what they are, must handle cases like yours with cruel dispatch. I am compelled to agree that death is the only possible sentence."

There were nods along the table, voices murmuring: "Yes, death—death—immediate—"

"Just a minute!" Hedrock's voice made a strong pattern

above the quiet medley. "Did you say that this council room is now a part of the hotel not previously occupied by the Meteor corporation?"

They stared at him blankly, as he ran, not waiting for a reply, straight at the ornamental panel on the darkly gleaming wall to his right. It was simpler than he had expected in his wildest imaginings. No one stopped him; no one even drew a gun. As he reached the panel, he adjusted his four fingers, accurately fitted them against the panel, twisted—and the ring slid out of its hidden groove on to his index finger. In one continuous, synchronized motion, he turned its pale-green fire on the vibratory device—and stepped through the transmitter.

Hedrock wasted no time examining the familiar room in which he found himself. It was located in underground vaults twenty-five hundred miles from Imperial City, filled with softly pulsing machines and glittering instruments. His hand closed on a wall switch. There was a hiss of power as he plunged it home. He had a brief mind picture, then, of all the rings and devices in the Hotel Royal Ganeel dissolving out of existence. They had served their purpose. One surprise escape was all he could ever hope to make from the Weapon Shops. He turned, walked through a door; and then, at the last instant, saw his deadly danger and tried to leap back.

Too late. The twenty-foot monster pounced on him. Its sledge-hammer paws sent him spinning along one wall, dizzy, sick, half unconscious. He tried to move, to rise—and saw the gigantic white rat darting toward him, its great teeth bared for the kill.

4

GRIMLY, HEDROCK WAITED UNTIL THE LAST POSSIBLE MOMENT. And then the roar of his voice filled the room with its threatening echoes. There was a massive squealing as the rat dodged aside into the far corner. It crouched there, and he could see that its violent movement had incremented its already speeded up life processes. Slowly, it began to keel over. Its glazed eyes peered at Hedrock as he staggered over to the rat enclosure, straight for the line of power switches. It made no effort to follow him; and, in a moment, he had pulled the lever that furnished the force for its size.

More slowly, he walked back into the large room. He had already noticed where the wall had been smashed but he did not pause to examine the break. It required half a minute to find the creature, now that it was no longer physically magnified. But he finally saw the six-inch glint of dirty white, where it had crawled under a broken chair. It was still alive, a very old-looking rat. It twisted weakly as he picked it up and carried it through the rat enclosure into the laboratory beyond. The feeling that came to him then had very little to do with the miserable creature he was placing in his data-gathering machine. It was pity, but on a vast scale, not for any individual. The compassion embraced all life. He felt, suddenly, alone in a world where people and things lived and died with heart-breaking rapidity, ephemeral shadows that blinked in the strong light from the sun, and then faded and were gone forevermore.

With an effort, he fought off that black mood and, turning away from the data machine, went to examine his rat enclosure. The four rat houses were doing well. Each had a new batch of young ones, and from the size of them he guessed that they had been born since the mechanical process had been interrupted by the rat that had broken out.

It would take too long to repair the break in the big metal pen, but the rest of the process resumed with automatic precision the moment he threw the switches back into position. The process was simplicity itself. He had begun it a thousand years before by introducing a dozen rats (six males and six females) into each of four specially constructed houses. Food was provided at intervals. The pens were kept clean by an ingenious pusher device that worked on a gear system. Nature had her own automatic methods, and every little while youngsters appeared and grew up, adding to the weight of the delicate balances that held up the floor. As soon as the weight of rats on the poised floor reached a set point, a little door would open, and sooner or later a rat would go into the narrow corridor beyond. The door would close behind it; and no other door in any of the four houses would open until it was disposed of. At the far end of the corridor was bait, inside which was a tiny Weapon Shop magnifier. When swallowed, the magnifier warmed from the rat's body heat and set off a relay which opened the door into an enclosure forty feet long, wide and high. It also set the little corridor floor moving. Like it or not, the rat was precipitated immediately into the open. That door shut too, blocking the way back.

More food in the center of the room activated the power that set off the magnifier. With a bang, the rat plummeted into size, becoming a twenty-foot monster, whose life functions speeded up in almost direct proportion to the difference in size. In that accelerated life-world, death came swiftly. And, as the corpse cooled below a certain temperature, the magnifying power was shut off, the floor tilted, and the small white body slid on to a conveyor belt which transported it to the data-gathering machine, from whence it was precipitated into a ray bath and disintegrated.

The process then repeated. And repeated and repeated and repeated. It had been going on for a millennium; and its purpose was tremendous. Somewhere along the line, the enlarging rays of the vibrator would do to a rat purposely what they had done accidentally to Hedrock fifty-five centuries previously. A rat would become immortal, and provide him with a priceless subject for experiment. Some day, if he succeeded in his search, all men would be immortal.

The data card of the rat that had so nearly killed him turned up in the "special" rack. There were three other cards with it, but the special quality about them was the continued functioning of some organ after death. Long ago, he had explored similar freak happenings to exhaustion. The fourth card excited Hedrock. The rat that had attacked him had lived the equivalent of ninety-five years. No wonder it had had time to break out. It must have lived several hours as a giant.

He calmed himself because he couldn't go into the matter now. The rat would have been precipitated, not into the dissolver, but into the preserver with the other specials, and would be waiting for his examination at some future date. Right now there were things to do, vitally important things affecting the existing human race; and he, who worked so hard for the future, had never yet let the might-be interfere at decisive moments with the *now*.

There were things to do, and they must be done before the Weapon Shop Council could completely nullify his position and his power in the Weapon Shop organization. Swiftly, Hedrock donned one of his "business" suits, and stepped through a transmitter.

He arrived in one of his secret apartments in Imperial City, and saw by his watch that ten minutes had passed since he had escaped from the Hotel Royal Ganeel. He'd be reasonably safe in assuming that the tens of thousands of Weapon Shop members would not yet have been notified that he was now regarded as a traitor. Hedrock seated himself at the apartment 'stat, and called the Weapon Shop information center.

"Hedrock speaking," he said when an operator answered. "Get me the address of Derd Kershaw."

"Yes, Mr. Hedrock." The response was quick and courteous, with no indication that his name was now anethema to the Shops. There was a pause, and then he heard the familiar click at the other end.

Another woman spoke, "I have Mr. Kershaw's file here, sir. Would you like it sent to you, or shall I read it to you?"

"Hold it up," said Hedrock, "I'll copy the information I want."

The image of a file sheet slid on to his 'stat plate. He noted down Kershaw's most recent address, "1874 Trellis Minor Building." The rest of "page" one was devoted to previous addresses of Kershaw, and to information about his birthplace, parentage, and the childhood trainings he had received.

There was a gold star stamped on the lower right corner of the "page". It was a Weapon Shop designation of merit, and indicated that Derd Kershaw was regarded by the shop scientists as one of the two or three greatest men in his field of physics.

"All right," said Hedrock, "next page, please."

The metal plate, many times thinner than an equal weight of paper, disappeared, and then reappeared again. "Page" two took up the story of Kershaw's life where the first page had left off. Teen-age training, college training, character and intelligence evaluations, early achievements, and finally lists of scientific discoveries and inventions.

Hedrock did not pause to read the list of Kershaw's discoveries. He could check on the details later. He had secured Kershaw's name from Edward Gonish, the No-man, and that was a stroke of luck that must not be lightly cancelled by any slow action now. Because of that accidental meeting he had information about which, he had reason to believe, no one else was as yet doing anything. It was true that Gonish did not regard his intuition about Kershaw and interstellar travel as complete. But his words provided a working basis. Accordingly for another hour, or even a day, Robert Hedrock could follow up the clue without interference from the shops.

"Turn to the last page," he said quickly. The page came on. Hedrock's gaze flashed to the list of names at the right. They were the names of individuals who had most recently made use of the file. There were only two names, Edward Gonish, and below that, Dan Neelan. He stared at the second name with narrowed eyes and because he was alert and keyed up he noticed something that he might ordinarily have missed. Behind the name of Gonish there had been stamped a tiny symbol. It indicated that the No-man had made use of the file and that it had subsequently been returned to its cabinet. There was no such symbol after the name of Neelan. He asked swiftly, "When did Nelan make use of this file, and who is he?"

34

The girl was calm. "Mr. Neelan's call is not completed, sir. When you requested the file we withdrew it from that section and transferred it over here. One minute, please. I'll connect you with the operator involved."

She spoke to someone Hedrock couldn't see and he did not catch her words. There was a pause and then another girl's face came on the 'statplate. The new operator nodded when she understood what was wanted. "Mr. Neelan," she said, "is waiting at this moment in the Linwood Avenue Weapon Shop. His first inquiry was about his brother, Gil Neelan, who, it seems, disappeared about a year ago. When we told him that his brother's last known address was the same as that of Derd Kershaw, he asked for information about Kershaw. We were in process of searching for that information when your call with its higher priority came through."

Hedrock said, "Then Neelan is still waiting at the Linwood shop?"

"Yes."

"Hold him there," said Hedrock, "until I can get to the shop. I am not in a position to use a transmitter so it will take about fifteen minutes."

The girl said, "We'll take our time giving him his information."

"Thank you," said Hedrock. And broke the connection.

Regretfully but swiftly Hedrock removed his "business" suit. He stepped with it back through the transmitter into the laboratory and then returned to the apartment. He dressed in a normal cloth suit and headed for the roof of the apartment block to the hangar where he kept a private carplane.

It was a model he hadn't used for several years, so precious minutes slid by while he checked the motor and the controls. In the air he had time to consider what he had done. What disturbed him most was the change from the "business" suit. And yet, there had been no alternative. The suit, which operated on the same energy principles as the "material" of which a weapon shop was made, was large enough to set up an energy disturbance in any part of the weapon shop, and was in its turn easily affected by the shop. Even that wouldn't matter particularly by itself. But the disturbance was dangerous when it occurred close to the skin. It was possible to carry Weapon Shop energy guns and ring devices into a shop without ill effects, but a "business" suit was impractically large. There was another unfortunate aspect to his wearing such a suit into a weapon shop. He had incorporated into it features and inventions not known to the Weapon Makers. The possibility that some of those secrets might be analysed by detector instruments was in itself sufficient reason for leaving the suit in

35

a safe place.

There was no sign of anything unusual as he approached the Linwood shop. His carplane was fitted with extremely sensitive detectors and if there had been a Weapon Shop warship hovering out of sight in the blue mists anywhere above the city they would have spotted it. That gave him, he estimated, a leeway of approximately five minutes, allowing for acceleration and deceleration of a spaceship in the atmosphere near the surface of the earth.

Hedrock brought his machine down beside the shop and glanced at his watch. Twenty-three minutes had passed since he had broken the 'stat connection with the Weapon Shop information center. And that meant it was now three quarters of an hour since his escape from the council room of the Weapon Makers. Warnings about him would be spreading farther through the vast organization. The time would come when the attendants of this weapon shop before him would also be advised. That put a pressure on him. And yet, despite the need for quick action, Hedrock stepped down from the carplane without haste and paused for another more searching examination of the shop. The usual sign glowed above it:

FINE WEAPONS

THE RIGHT TO BUY WEAPONS IS THE RIGHT TO

BE FREE

Like all similar glitter signs, it seemed to turn to face him as he walked toward it. The illusion was one of the commoner aspects of a main thoroughfare, and yet a few hundred such signs could make so dazzling a spectacle that people had been known to become light-intoxicated. It was a pleasant experience, with colors and the sensation of floating on air, and no dangerous after effects. There was a pill you could take to normalize the vision centers quickly.

The shop stood in a glade of green and floral vegetation. It made a restful and idyllic picture in its garden-like setting. It all seemed very normal and as of old. The window sign when he approached it was the same as it had always been. The letters were smaller than those on the outside sign, but the words were equally positive:

THE FINEST ENERGY WEAPONS

IN THE KNOWN UNIVERSE

Hedrock knew that that was true. He gazed at the gleaming display of revolvers and rifles and he was briefly shocked to realize that more than 100 years had passed since he had last visited a weapon shop. It made the shop itself more interesting than it might otherwise have been. He had a sudden awareness

36

of what a wonderful organization the Weapon Makers were, with their shops existing in tens of thousands of cities and towns in the far-flung Isher Empire, an independent, outlawed, indestructible, altruistic opposition to tyranny. It was sometimes hard to believe that every weapon shop was an impregnable fort and that bloodily earnest attempts had been made by the Isher governments in the past to smash the organization.

Hedrock walked quickly now toward the door. It wouldn't open when he pulled at it. He let go, and stared at it, startled. And then he realized what was the matter. The sensitive door was condemning him because there were so many thoughts near the surface of his mind of the action taken against him by the Weapon Shop council. The door worked by thought and no enemy of the Shops, no servant of the Empress, had ever been admitted.

He closed his eyes and let himself relax, let all the tense thoughts of the past hour drain from him. Presently, he tried the door again.

It opened gently, like a flower unfolding its petals, only faster. It was weightless in his fingers, like some supernally delicate and insubstantial structure, and when he stepped through the opening it crowded his heels without touching them and closed behind him silently as a night in space.

Hedrock stepped gingerly through a little alcove into a larger room.

5

IT WAS QUIET INSIDE. NOT A SOUND PENETRATED FROM the busy daylight world from which he had come. His eyes swiftly accustomed themselves to the soft lighting, which came like a reflection from the walls and ceiling. He glanced around alertly, and at first he had the impression that there was no one in the outer room. That tensed him, for it seemed to indicate that they had been unable to hold Neelan.

It might even be that the expected warning had come through, and that this was a trap.

Hedrock sighed, and relaxed. Because if it was a trap then his chances of escape would depend on how many men they were prepared to sacrifice. They must know he would fight to avoid capture. On the other hand, if it was not a trap there was nothing to worry about.

He decided not to worry, for a time anyway.

He gazed curiously at the showcases which stood against the walls or were neatly arranged around the floor. They were shining structures, about a dozen of them altogether. Hedrock stepped up to the one nearest the door, and gazed at the four rifles that were mounted inside it. The sight of them thrilled him. He had had much to do with the development of these intricate energy weapons, but with him familiarity with machines had never bred contempt.

Many of these weapons still carried the old names. "Guns" they were called, or "revolvers," or "rifles," but there the resemblance ended. These "guns" did not shoot bullets, they discharged energy in many forms and quantities. Some of them could kill or destroy at a thousand miles if necessary, and yet they were controlled by the same sensitive elements as the weapon shop door. Just as the door refused to open for police officers, Imperial soldiers or people unfriendly to the Shops, so these guns had been set to fire only in self-defence, and against certain animals during open season.

They also had other special qualities, particularly as to defence and speed of operation.

Hedrock moved around the edge of the case, and saw that there was a tall man sitting in a chair almost out of sight behind another showcase. He presumed it was Neelan, but before he could go over and introduce himself, there was an interruption. The door to the rear of the shop opened, and an older, heavily built man emerged. He came forward with an apologetic smile on his lips.

"I beg your pardon, Mr. Hedrock," he said. "I was aware of the outer door opening, and guessed it was you. But I had started a mechanical operation which I could not leave."

He was still being treated as if he was a major Weapon Shop personage. Hedrock gave the attendant one sharp glance, and decided that the man had not yet been advised that Robert Hedrock no longer had Weapon Shop privileges. The attendant raised his voice, "Oh, Mr. Neelan, this is the gentleman I mentioned to you."

The stranger climbed to his feet, as Hedrock and the clerk came over. The clerk said, "I took the liberty of informing Mr. Neelan a few minutes ago that you were coming." He broke off. "Mr. Neelan, I want you to meet Robert Hedrock, an executive officer of the Weapon Shops."

As they shook hands, Hedrock was aware of himself being examined by a pair of hard, black eyes. Neelan's face was heavily tanned, and Hedrock guessed that he had recently been to planets or on meteors that had little or no protection from the direct rays of the sun.

He began to regret that he had not taken the time to find out a little more about Dan Neelan and his missing brother. Having failed to do so, the important thing now was to take Neelan out of the shop to a place where they could talk in safety. Before he could speak, the attendant said: "For your information, Mr. Hedrock, we are securing Mr. Neelan's mail for him from his Martian postal address. You'll have plenty of time to talk to him."

Hedrock did not argue the matter. The words had a fateful clang. But what had happened was natural enough. The women at Information Center had sought a simple solution to the problem of holding Neelan for him in this shop. So they had offered to secure his mail from Mars by way of a Weapon Shop transmitter.

They had set a limited objective, and they had achieved it. It was possible that Neelan could be lured out of the shop for a short time. But there was a stubborn twist to the man's lips, and his eyes were ever so faintly narrowed, as if he had had to accustom himself to watch for trickery. Hedrock knew that breed of men, and it was unwise to try to put them under pressure. A suggestion to leave the shop would have to wait, but the need for speed could be indicated. He turned to the attendant.

"Great issues are at stake, so I hope you won't think me impolite if I start to talk immediately to Mr. Neelan."

The older man smiled. "I'll leave you two alone," he said, and went into the back room.

There was another chair in a nearby corner. Hedrock dragged it over, motioned Neelan back into his own chair, and settled down himself. He began immediately: "I'm going to be very frank with you, Mr. Neelan. The Weapon Shops have reason to believe that Derd Kershaw and your brother have invented an interstellar drive. There is evidence that the Empress of Isher would be unalterably opposed to the release of such an invention. And, accordingly, Kershaw and your brother are in serious danger of being killed and imprisoned. It's vitally important to find out where they were building this drive and what has happened to them." He finished quietly, "I hope you will be able to tell me what you know of the affair."

Neelan was shaking his head. His smile was ironic, almost grim. "My brother is in no danger of being killed," he said.

"Then you know where he is?" Hedrock was relieved.

Neelan hesitated. When he finally spoke, Hedrock had the feeling that the words were not those that the man had first intended to utter. Neelan said, "What do you want of me?"

"Well, for one thing, who are you?"

39

The determined face relaxed the faintest bit. "My name is Daniel Neelan. I am the twin brother of Gilbert Neelan. We were born in Lakeside . . . Is that what you mean?"

Hedrock smiled his friendliest smile. "A development of that. There are lines in your face that indicate a lot has happened since then."

"Right now," said Neelan, "I could be classified as a meteor miner. For the past ten years I've been away from earth. Most of that time I spent as a gambler on Mars, but two years ago I won a meteorite from a drunken fellow named Carew. I gave him back half of it out of pity, and we became partners. The meteor is three miles in diameter, and it's practically a solid chunk of 'heavy' beryllium. On paper we're worth billions of credits, but it needs another couple of years of development before we can start to cash in. About a year ago I had a very special reason for believing that something had happened to my brother."

He paused. There was an odd expression on his face. Finally, he said, "Have you ever heard of the experiments conducted by the Eugenics Institute?"

"Why, yes," said Hedrock, with the beginning of understanding. "Some remarkable work has been done, particularly with identical twins."

Neelan nodded. "That makes it easier to tell you what happened."

He stopped again, and then slowly began his account. The scientists had taken them at the age of five, Daniel and Gilbert Neelan, identical twins already sensitive to each other, and magnified the sensitivity until it was a warm interflow of life force, a world of dual sensation. The interrelation grew so sharp that at short distances, thought passed between them with all the clarity of the electronic flux in a local telestat.

Those early years had been pure joy of intimate relation. And then at the age of twelve began the attempt to make them different without breaking the nervous connection. Like a kid tossed into a deep pool to sink or swim, he was subjected to the full impact of Isher civilization, while Gil was secluded and confined to studious ways. Over those years, their intellectual association declined. Thoughts, though still transmittable, could be concealed. Neelan developed a curiously strong, big-brother attitude toward Gil, while Gil—

The grim man paused in his account, glanced at Hedrock, and then continued, "I guess I noticed the diffident way in which Gil tackled adulthood by the way he reacted to my experiences with taking out women. It shocked him, and so I began to realize that we had a problem." He shrugged. "There never was any question as to which of us would leave Earth.

40

On the day that the contract with the Eugenics Institute terminated, I bought a ticket for Mars. I went there in the belief that Gil would have his chance at life. Only—" he finished in a drab voice "—it turned out to be death."

"Death?" said Hedrock.

"Death."

"When?"

"A year ago. That's what brought me to Earth. I was on the meteor when I *felt* him die."

Hedrock said, "It's taken you a long time to get here." The remark sounded too sharp, so he added quickly, "Please understand, I'm only trying to obtain a clear picture."

Neelan said wearily, "We were caught on the far side of the sun, because the meteor's velocity almost matched that of Earth. It only recently came into a position where we could figure out an acceptable orbit for our simple type freighter. A week ago Carew set me down at one of the cheap northern spaceports. He departed at once, but he's due to pick me up in about six months."

Hedrock nodded. The account was satisfactory. "Just what did you feel when your brother died?" he asked.

Neelan shifted in his chair. There had been pain, he explained uneasily. Gil had died in agony, suddenly, without expecting it. The anguish had bridged the multimiles between Earth and the meteor, and twisted his own nerves in dreadful sympathy. Instantly, there had been an end to that neutral pressure which had constituted, even at that distance, the bond between his brother and himself.

He finished, "I haven't felt so much as a tingle since then."

In the silence that followed, Hedrock realized that his time must be running short.

For minutes the necessity for concentrating on Neelan's words had kept the pressure of urgency away from his mind. Now that barrier was no more, and the pressure was on. Time to leave! Leave now! The purpose was steady and intense; and because of his sharp awareness of things Weapon Shop he knew that he dared not ignore the warning impulse. And yet —he leaned back in his chair, and stared at the other man soberly. When he departed he wanted to take Neelan with him, and that meant the process must be orderly. He made a mental calculation, and slowly shook his head.

"I can't quite see this affair as having gone through a major crisis as far back as a year ago."

Neelan's black eyes were suddenly dull as tarnished metal. "I've noticed that the death of one man seldom produces a crisis," he said in a drab voice. "I hate to say that in connection with my own brother, but it's the truth."

41

"And yet," said Hedrock, "something happened. For Kershaw is also missing."

He did not wait for a reply, but climbed to his feet and walked to the control board, which was located on the wall to his left. All these minutes he had been acutely conscious that Weapon Shop soldiers might swarm through the transmitter that was there. He couldn't take the chance of that happening while he was organizing his retreat.

He stepped close to the board, with its winking lights. He intended to make sure Neelan couldn't see what he was doing. Quickly, he activated one of his rings, and burned a needle-small hole in the delicate transmitter circuit. Instantly, a tiny light behind the paneling went dead.

Hedrock turned away from the board, relieved but as intent on his purpose as ever. He had protected his flank, nothing more. There was another transmitter in the rear of the shop, and for all he knew men were coming through it at this very moment. And other men in armored warships could be swinging in to cut him off from his carplane.

The risks he was taking were measured in just such desperate terms. He walked back to Neelan, and said, "I have an address of your brother's that I'd like to check right away. And I want you to come with me." He spoke earnestly. "I assure you speed is important. You can tell me the rest of your story on the way, and I can drop you back here afterwards to pick up your mail."

Neelan stood up. "Actually, there's not very much more to tell," he said. "When I arrived in Imperial City, I located my brother's old address, and learned something that—"

"Just a moment," said Hedrock. He walked to the door that led to the rear, knocked on it, and called, "I'm taking Mr. Neelan with me, but he'll be back for his mail. Thank you for your cooperation."

He didn't wait for a reply, but returned to Neelan. "Let's go," he said briskly.

Neelan headed for the front entrance, talking as he went. "I discovered that my brother had maintained a false residence for registration purposes."

As they were going out of the door, Hedrock said, "You mean he didn't live at his registered address?"

"His landlady told me," said Neelan, "that he not only didn't live there, but gave her permission to rent the room. He turned up one evening a month, as required by law, and so her conscience was clear."

Out of the shop and along the walk that led toward the carplane.... Hedrock knew that Neelan was talking, and presently the meaning would penetrate. But his attention now was on the heavens. Planes flitted across them, but no long dark shape; no torpedo-like structure darting in on wings of atomic energy. . . . He held the door of his small machine open for Neelan, and stepped in after him. A moment later, he sank into the control chair; and from its vantage point saw that there was no movement around the shop.

As the carplane climbed into the air Hedrock saw that Neelan was examining the controls. There was a confidence about his exploration that spoke "expert" louder than words. The man caught his gaze, and said, "There're a couple of new things here. What's this gadget?" He indicated the detector system.

That particular device was a Weapon Shop secret. It was not a very important one, however, so Hedrock had risked putting it in a plane that could conceivably fall into the hands of people hostile to the Shops. The Imperial government had similar devices but of slightly different construction.

Hedrock countered Neelan's question. "I see you're familiar with machinery?"

"I majored in atomic engineering," said Neelan. He added with a faint smile, "The Eugenic Institute does well by its protegés."

In this case, they had indeed. Until this instant Hedrock had considered Neelan important because of the information he might have. He was impressed by the obviously tough fiber of the other's character, but he had met so many hard and capable men in his long career that that quality of itself had not seemed of outstanding interest. The degree was. It changed his attitude. A man who knew atomic energy in the all embracing way it was taught at the great universities could practically name his own price if he went into industry. And if they ever found the interstellar drive he'd be of inestimable value. Accordingly, Neelan was a man to be cultivated. Hedrock began at once. He drew out of his pocket the slip of paper that had Kershaw's last known address written on it. He handed it to Neelan with the remark, "That's where we're heading."

Neelan took the paper, and read it aloud, "Room 1874, Trellis Minor building—Good God!"

"What's the matter?"

"I've been there three times," said Neelan. "I found the address in a suitcase my brother kept at the boarding house."

Hedrock could almost feel his search coming to a dead stop. Nevertheless, his comment went unerringly to the root of the other's words, "*Three* times?" he said.

"It's a room," Neelan said. "Every time I went there the door was locked. The building manager told me the rent had been paid ten years in advance, but that he hadn't seen any-one there since the contract was signed. That was three years ago."

"But you didn't go in?"

"No, he wouldn't let me, and I had no desire to get put in jail. And, besides, I don't think I could have gotten in. The lock was a protected one."

Hedrock nodded thoughtfully. He had no intention of letting any lock stop him. But he could appreciate the obstacle that such devices presented to even the most determined men who lacked his facilities. There was another thought in his mind. Somewhere along here he would have to drop in at one of his apartments and don his "business" suit. It was desperately important that he protect himself, and yet, so long as the Weapon Shops could trace his movements he dared not slow his pace. In the final issue the half it would take to secure his own safety might make all the difference. Even a ten minute advantage in time could be decisive.

The risks involved had to be taken.

They came to where a hundred story building flashed up at them the sign: TRELLIS MAJOR BUILDING. The wrongness of the name did not immediately strike Hedrock. He was only a few hundred yards above the stupendous structure when he saw the smaller, fifty story, spired monster that was the Trellis Minor Building. The sight jarred his memory. He recalled for the first time that Trellis Major and Minor were two meteors revolving around each other somewhere beyond Mars. The larger was contraterrene matter, the smaller terrene. They were being mined assiduously by a single company; and these massive buildings were but two by-products of the still un-ended treasure that flowed in a steady stream from that remote region of solar space.

Hedrock guided the carplane to a roof landing on the smaller building, and the two of them took an elevator down to the eighteenth floor. Hedrock needed only one glance at the outside of room 1874 to realize that it was indeed well protected. The door and its frame were of a steel-strong aluminium alloy. The lock was an electronic tube, and there was printing on it which read, "When tampered with, this lock mechanism flashes warnings in the office of the building manager, the local police station, and on all passing patrol planes."

The Weapon Shops had developed a dozen devices to circumvent such electronic circuits. The best one was the least complicated. It involved absolute faith in a curious characteristic of matter and energy. If a circuit was broken—or established—swiftly enough (the speeds involved were faster than

44

light) the current would, in the former instance, continue to flow just as if there had been no break, and in the latter would establish a flow between two distant points in space just as if there was no distance. The phenomenon was no minor incident of science. The intricate matter transmitter that had made the Weapon Shops possible was based on it.

Hedrock motioned Neelan back, and stepped close to the door. He used a different ring this time, and a glow of orange flame reflected for several feet from the point of contact. The light died into nothingness, and he shoved at the door. It opened with a faint squeal of its long unused hinges. Hedrock stepped across the threshold into an office twenty feet long by ten wide. There was a desk at one end, and several chairs as well as a small filing cabinet. In the corner beside the desk was a telestat, its plate blank and lifeless.

The room was so bare, so obviously unlived in and unused that Hedrock walked forward a short distance and then stopped. Involuntarily, he turned to glance back at Neelan. The gambler was bending down beside the lock, studying it thoughtfully. He looked up at Hedrock, and shook his head wonderingly. "How did you do that?"

It cost Hedrock a mental effort to realize that the other was referring to the way he had opened the door. He smiled, then said gravely, "I'm sorry, that's a secret." He added quickly, "Better come inside. We don't want to rouse anyone's suspicions."

Neelan straightened with alacrity, stepped into the room and closed the door. Hedrock said, "You take the desk, and I'll examine the file cabinets. The faster we do this the better I'll like it."

His own job was over in less than a minute. The file drawers were empty. He pushed the last one shut, and walked over to the desk. Neelan was peering into a bottom drawer, and Hedrock saw instantly that it was empty also. Neelan closed the drawer, and stood up.

"That's it," he said. "What now?"

Hedrock did not reply immediately. There were things that could still be done. There were probably new leads to be found in the terms of the lease under which the room had been rented. A check-up could be made with the telestat company. What calls had been made from and to this office? Given time, he could probably re-establish a very solid trail.

That was the trouble. Time was the one thing he didn't have. Once more, standing there, he was amazed that the Weapon Shops had not caught up to him long before this. In the days when he had been head of the coordination department, he'd have had his facts about Kershaw within minutes

45

of the first notification from the council. It seemed incredible that his successor, the able and brilliant No-man trainee, John Hale, was not equally successful. Whatever the meaning of the delay, it couldn't possibly last much longer. The sooner he departed the better.

He turned and started for the door. And stopped. Because if he left now where else would he go? Slowly, then, he straightened and faced the room again. Perhaps his search hadn't been quite thorough enough. Perhaps in his anxiety he had overlooked the obvious.

He would remain and find out.

At first there was nothing. As his gaze moved from the window behind the desk, he rejected each object in turn: the desk with its empty drawers; the filing cabinet, also empty; the chairs, the room itself, barren except for a minimum of furniture and no mechanisms except a telestat. He paused there. "Telestat," he said out loud. "Why, of course."

He started towards it, and then stopped as he grew aware of Neelan's eyes following him questioningly. "Quick," he said, "against the wall." He motioned to the area behind the 'stat. "I don't think he should see you."

"Who?" said Neelan. But he must have been convinced, for he walked to the indicated position.

Hedrock switched on the 'stat. He was furious at himself for not having made the test on entering the room. For years he had lived in the Weapon Shop world of channeled 'stats, 'stats that were connected only in series, 'stats that did not have dial systems, and he had lived in his own secret world of private, building-to-building 'stats. And therefore his slow understanding of the possibilities of *this* 'stat was almost a form of suicide.

A minute passed, and the plate remained blank. Two minutes—was that a sound? He couldn't be sure, but it seemed to be coming from the speaker, a padded movement as of—that was it—footsteps. They stopped abruptly, and there was silence. Hedrock tried to visualize a man staring uncertainly down at it undecided about answering it. The third minute went by. The sense of defeat began to weigh on him, for these were priceless minutes that were passing.

At the end of five minutes, a man's harsh voice said, "Yes, what is it?"

The thrill of that reached clear down to Hedrock's toes. He had his story prepared, but before he could reply the voice spoke again, more sharply, "Are you answering the ad? They told me it couldn't go in till tomorrow. Why didn't they ring me up and tell me they'd be able to get it in today?"

He sounded furious, and once more he failed to wait for a

reply. "Are you an atomic engineer?" he asked.

"Yes," said Hedrock.

It was easy to say. The swift way the other had jumped to a false conclusion made it as simple as that to change the story he had organized. His intention had been to pass himself off as Dan Neelan and explain that he had found the address of this office in his brother's personal effects. He had had in mind to be callous about his brother's death, and take the attitude that his interest was in the estate. It had seemed reasonable to him, and still seemed so, that the reaction to such a frank account would be highly significant. It would either show friendly awareness of Gil Neelan's brother—in which case he'd tone down the callousness—or unfriendly awareness. And if there was no recognition at all, that also would have a meaning.

He waited, but not for long this time. "You must," said the voice from the telestat, "be wondering the why of this queer method of employment."

Hedrock felt vaguely sorry for the man. The other was so sharply conscious of the queerness of his own actions that he took it for granted that everyone else was conscious of them also. The best method of dealing with such a projection was to play along with it. "I did wonder," he said, "but I don't really give a damn."

The man laughed, not too pleasantly. "Glad to hear that. I've got a job here that'll take just about two months; and I'll pay you eight hundred credits a week, and no questions asked. How's that?"

More and more curious, Hedrock thought. It was a moment when caution would seem reasonable. He said slowly, "What is it you want me to do?"

"Just what the ad said. Repair atomic motors. Well—" Peremptorily "—what do you say?"

Hedrock asked *the* question. "Where do I report?"

There was silence. "Not so fast," the answer came at last. "I'm not going to hand out a lot of information, and then you not take the job. You realize that I'm paying you twice the going rate? Are you interested?"

"It's just the kind of job I'm looking for," said Hedrock.

He felt remote from the illegality that seemed to lie behind the other's carefulness. Even Neelan's problem was only incidental. There would be details of murder to investigate, but he who had watched generations of human beings die could never be too concerned with a few more dead men. His purposes were on a different level.

The voice was saying, "Five blocks north along 131st Street. Then about nine blocks east to 1997 232nd Avenue, Center,

47

It's a tall, narrow, grayish building. You can't miss it. Ring the bell, and wait for an answer. Get that?"

Hedrock wrote the precious address down swiftly. "Got it," he said finally. "When shall I report?"

"Right away." The voice was threatening. "Understand me, I don't want you rushing off somewhere else. If you want this job you'll come over by public carplane, and I know just how long it will take, so don't try to fool me. I expect you over here in about ten minutes."

Hedrock thought, "My God. Am I never going to get back to my apartment?"

Aloud he said, "I'll be there."

He waited. The 'stat plate remained blank. Evidently, the other man was not interested in seeing what the applicant looked like. Abruptly, there was a click, and he knew that the connection had been broken.

The interview was over.

Quickly, he used one of his rings to insure that the telestat would not be used by anyone else—and turned as Neelan came forward. He was smiling, a lithely built man, almost as tall, almost as big as Hedrock himself. "Good work," he said. "That was a smooth job. What was that address again? Ninety-seven what street?"

Hedrock said, "Let's get out of here."

His mind worked swiftly as they walked rapidly to the elevator. He had been wondering what he was going to do with Neelan. The man was valuable and might prove to be a wonderful ally for a normally lone operator like himself. But it was too soon to take him into confidence. Besides, there wasn't time to make the detailed story out of it that would be necessary to gain Neelan's support.

As their elevator raced towards the roof, Hedrock said, "My idea is that you go back to the Linwood shop and pick up your mail, while I go and see the unpleasant individual I talked to. Afterwards rent a room at the Hotel Isher—I'll call you there. That way we'll do both jobs in half the time."

There was more to it than that. The sooner Neelan returned to the Weapon Shop the greater the likelihood that he would get there before the Weapon Shop search team. And if he waited in a hotel instead of his room, it would take just so much longer for any searchers to locate him. His failure to remember the address the voice had given made sending him considerably less dangerous.

Neelan was speaking. "You can drop me off at the first public carplane platform. But what about that address?"

"I'll write it for you as soon as we get on my ship," said Hedrock.

They were on the roof now, and he had a moment of terrible tension as several carplanes swooped down and landed with a rush. But the men and women who climbed out of them paid no attention to the two men heading for the carplane on the north runway.

As soon as they were up in the air, Hedrock saw the flashing sign of a carplane platform. He dived towards it, and simultaneously pulled a slip of paper towards him, and wrote, "97 131st Street." A moment later they were on the pavement. He folded the paper, and gave it to Neelan as the latter climbed out of the carplane. They shook hands.

"Good luck," said Neelan.

"Don't go back to your brother's room," said Hedrock.

He hurried back to the control chair, closed the door, and instants later manipulated his machine above the traffic. Through the rear view plate of the control board, he watched Neelan climb aboard a public carplane. It was impossible to tell whether he was aware that he had been given the wrong address.

The Weapon Shop experts could use associative techniques to get the real one out of him, of course. He undoubtedly remembered it on some level of awareness. But it would take time to persuade him to cooperate, and time to induce the necessary associations. Hedrock actually had no objection to the Shops having the information. As he guided his machine slowly towards the address given him by the voice, he wrote another, longer note, with the real address on it. This one he placed in an envelope. On the envelope he wrote: *Peter Cadron, The Meteor Corporation, Hotel Ganeel, Imperial City— Deliver noon mail, the 6th.* That was tomorrow.

Under normal circumstances he would have been working with the Shops. Their purposes were basically his also, and it was unfortunate that the entire council had allowed itself to be frightened by one man, himself. But they had, and the emotion might conceivably interfere with their efficiency. Their very slowness in following up the Kershaw lead seemed to prove that their action had already endangered their cause. Hedrock had no doubts about what he was doing. In a crisis he trusted himself. Other people were skilful and brave, but they lacked his vast experience, and his willingness to take prolonged risks.

It was possible that he was the only one as yet who really believed that this was one of the great crises of the critical reign of Innelda Isher. In the final issue a few minutes might make all the difference between success or failure. No one was better equipped than he to make those minutes count.

His plane crossed 232nd Avenue, Center, and he brought it

down in a carplane parking area on 233rd. He walked swiftly to the nearest corner, and mailed his letter, and then, satisfied, proceeded on to his destination. It was, he saw by his watch, exactly eleven minutes since he had talked to his prospective employer. Not too long.

So that was the building! Hedrock continued walking, but he studied it with a frown. It was an ungainly structure in that it was out of proportion, much too long for its width. Like a great, gray dull needle it poked into the lowering sky three, four hundred feet, a curiously sinister construction. There was no sign outside it to indicate what went on inside, simply a narrow walk leading from the sidewalk to a single, unimposing door that was level with the street. As he rang the doorbell, he tried to visualize Gilbert Neelan walking along this street on the day of his death, striding forward up to the door and disappearing forever. The mental picture did not seem complete, and he was still considering it when the now familiar harsh voice said from a hidden speaker above the door:

"You took your time about arriving."

Hedrock said steadily, "I came straight here."

There was a brief silence. Hedrock imagined the man measuring in his mind the distance from the Trellis Minor Building. The result seemed to be satisfactory, for he spoke again:

"Just a minute."

The door began to open. Hedrock saw a wide, high alcove, just how high he couldn't make out from where he was standing. He forgot the alcove as he found himself staring at a thick, partly open door made of dark, mottled metal. The entire inner wall, in which the big door was set, was smoothly wrought in the same metal. Hedrock stepped through the outer door, and paused as he realized what the over-all unnatural effect was. The inner wall was Fursching steel, the structural alloy that was used exclusively for the superhard shells of spaceships.

The strange building was a hangar for a spaceship. And the ship was *in*.

Kershaw's ship! It was a guess, but the speed with which he was moving required that he act as if all his guesses and assumptions were realities. Subsidiary thoughts raced through his mind. Gil Neelan, the brother of Dan, had not died on earth but in a flight through space. Which would seem to mean that the interstellar drive had been tested a whole year before. But, then, why were the people aboard acting as they did? Surely, Kershaw, the inventor would not be cowering nervously inside because somebody had been killed in an experiment, or because he was afraid of the Empress? He must

50

know that he could obtain the assistance of the Weapon Shops. All starred scientists were secretly advised that the "open" facilities of the Shops were available to them. On rare occasions even "confidential" information had been given certain trusted men.

Poised there, Hedrock guessed grimly that Kershaw also was dead. His thoughts grew even swifter, and turned now toward decisive action. Should he try to get inside while he had the opportunity? Or retreat to go after the precious "business" suit?

The questions almost answered themselves. If he left now, he would arouse the suspicions of the man to whom he had talked. If he remained and seized the ship, the entire problem of the drive would be solved.

"What's the matter?" The harsh voice came as he reached that point in his thoughts. "What are you waiting for? The door's open."

So he was already suspicious. But there was anxiety in his tone, also. This man, whoever he was, was definitely eager to have an atomic engineer come aboard. It placed him subtly in Hedrock's control. It made it possible for Hedrock to say truthfully: "I've just discovered that this is a spaceship. I don't want to leave earth."

"Oh!" There was silence. Then the voice said urgently, "Just a minute. I'll be right out. I'll prove to you that everything is as it should be. The ship can't fly till the motors have been gone over."

Hedrock waited. He had an idea that the proof was going to involve a gun. The question was, how big would it be? Not that it made any difference. He was going in, even if at the beginning he was at a disadvantage. Sooner or later his ring weapons would give him the opportunity he needed. As he watched, the inner door that had been fractionally open, swung wide. It revealed a third door, which was also open, and beyond that, floating in the air, was a mobile energy gun, mounted and riding easily on antigravity plates. The three-noded muzzle of the gun pointed with a mechanical steadiness at Hedrock. From an inner speaker, the man said in a tight, hard voice:

"You probably carry a Weapon Shop gun. I hope you realize the futility of such a weapon against a ninety-thousand cycle unit. Just toss your revolver through the door."

Hedrock, who did not carry ordinary guns, said, "I'm unarmed."

"Open your coat." Suspiciously.

Hedrock did so. There was silence, then, "All right, come on in."

Without a word, Hedrock stepped through the two inner doors, each of which, in turn, clanged behind him with heavy finality.

6

AS HEDROCK ADVANCED, THE GUN WITHDREW SIDEWAYS, and he had a kaleidoscope of swift impressions. He saw that he was in the control room of the spaceship, and that was startling. A control room was, by law, located in the center of a ship. That meant this hangar extended about four hundred feet underground, as well as above. This was an eight-hundred foot spaceship, a veritable monster.

"Well," the stranger's voice cut raspingly across his thought, "what do you think of it?"

Slowly, Hedrock turned toward his captor. He saw a long, pale-faced individual, about thirty-five years old. The man had maneuvered the mobile unit toward the ceiling, and he was standing behind a transparent energy insulator. He regarded Hedrock with large, brown, suspicious eyes. Hedrock said, "I can see there's something damn funny going on here. But I happen to need money quick, so I'll take the job. Does that make sense?"

He had struck, he realized, the right note. The man relaxed visibly. He smiled wanly. He spoke finally with an attempt at heartiness that didn't quite come off. "Now you're talking. You can see how it was. I thought you weren't going to come in."

Hedrock said, "The spaceship startled me, located here in the heart of the city." It was a point, it seemed to him, that he should press hard. The fact that all this was new and strange to him would emphasize that he had no advance knowledge of the existence of a spaceship. He went on, "So long as we understand each other, I guess we'll get along. The eight hundred credits a week still goes, does it?"

The man nodded. "And it'll be clear, too," he said, "because I'm taking no chances on you not coming back here."

Hedrock said, "What do you mean?"

The man smiled sardonically. He seemed to be more pleased with the situation. His voice sounded cool and confident as he said, "You're going to live aboard till the job is done."

Hedrock was not surprised. But he made a protest as a

matter of principle. He said, "Now, look here, I don't really mind staying aboard, but you're taking a pretty high-handed manner. What's up? It's all very well for me to keep saying it's none of my business. But every few seconds you keep pushing something new at me until—well, I think I have a right to a few general facts."

"Like hell you have," the man snapped.

Hedrock persisted, "What's your name? I don't think it will hurt you if I know who you are."

There was a pause. The other's long face twisted into a frown. He shrugged finally. "I guess I can tell you my name." He smiled with a sudden savage exultation. "After all, *she* knows it. My name is Rel Greer."

It meant nothing, except that it wasn't Kershaw. Hedrock didn't have to be told who *she* might be. Before he could speak, Greer said curtly: "Come along! I want you to change your clothes. Over there." He must have noticed Hedrock's almost imperceptible hesitation. "Or maybe," he sneered, "you're too modest to undress out in the open."

"I'm not modest," said Hedrock.

He walked over and picked up the work clothes he was supposed to change into, and he was thinking, *Shall I take a chance and keep my rings on? Or take them off?*

He looked up, and said aloud, "I'd like to examine this insulated suit before I put it on."

"Go ahead. It's your funeral if there's anything wrong with it."

"Exactly," said Hedrock.

The interchange, brief though it was, had already brought him a vital piece of information. He had taken one glance at the suit, and recognized that it was in good repair. These insulated suits for atomic workers had a long history; if anything went wrong they lost their gloss. This one positively shone; and Greer's casual acceptance of his suggestion that he examine it seemed to signify that the man didn't know anything about such things. The implications were tremendous. As he went over the material, Hedrock's mind was busy. Greer had indicated that the ship was not capable of flight. If that were true it could only mean that the motors had been taken apart. And that there was an uncomfortably large amount of radiation flooding the engine room. Because of the decision he had to make, it was a point that needed checking. He looked up, and asked the question.

Greer nodded, but there was a wary expression in his eyes. He said, "Yes, I took them apart, and then I realized the job was more than I cared to undertake."

That sounded reasonable enough, but Hedrock chose to

misunderstand. "I don't get that. The work is simple enough."

Greer shrugged. "I just didn't want to be bothered."

Hedrock said, "I never heard of an authorized trade school —let alone a college—graduating an atomic motor repairman who couldn't put an engine together again. Where did you get your training?"

Greer was impatient. "Look," he said flatly, "get into that suit."

Hedrock undressed quickly. He was not satisfied with the results of his attempt to find out how good a mechanic Greer was. But the brief conversation gave direction to the decision he had to make. If there was free radiation in the engine room, then he couldn't take his rings with him. An insulation suit was efficient only if there was no metal inside it; and, while it was possible that he might be able to use his rings against Greer before there was any danger, the risk was too great. It was much safer to slip the tiny weapons into a pocket of his suit just as if they were simple ornaments. There would be other opportunities to use them.

It required only a few moments to change his clothes. It was he who led the way down into the bowels of the ship.

They came to a world of engines.

He saw that Greer was enjoying his astonishment. "The ship is a new invention," he said smugly. "I'm selling it. I'm negotiating, and have been for some weeks, with the Empress herself." His lips tightened, then he went on, "I decided to tell you that on the way down. It isn't any of your business, but I don't want you worrying your head about it, and maybe prowling around. Now you know where you stand. It's *her* idea that the whole thing be kept quiet. And I pity any interloper who goes counter to her wishes in anything. The Earth wouldn't be big enough to hold such a fool unless he were a Weapon Shop man. There, is everything clear?"

It was much clearer than Greer realized. The great scientist, Kershaw, had hired Gil Neelan and Greer and others whose names had not yet been mentioned to assist him in perfecting his invention. Somewhere along the line Greer had murdered everyone else aboard, and taken control of the ship.

Hedrock climbed out of the engine room and up to the repair shop on the level above. He began to examine the tools, aware of Greer watching him. In turn, but much more casually, he watched Greer. Once more he was testing to discover just how much the man knew. Greer spoke again at last:

"I've fixed a place for myself in the empty room above this repair shop. I'll spend most of my time there during the next two months. It isn't that I don't trust you, or that there is very much you can do. But while I'm up there I'll *know* that you're not wandering around the ship, prying into secrets."

Hedrock said nothing. He did not quite trust himself to speak, for fear that he would say too much to a man who had now irrevocably revealed himself. Greer was obviously not a scientist. And in a few minutes, as soon as he climbed up to the chamber above, the problem of seizing the ship would be solved.

The irritating thing, then, was that Greer didn't go up to the next level right away.

He had another reason for wanting the man to depart. One of the amazing aspects of his various interchanges with Greer was that the other had not yet asked him for his name. Hedrock had no intention of saying that he was Gilbert Neelan; he intended to claim that the whole situation was too unnormal for him to reveal his identity. But still that might make for unpleasantness and delay.

Greer broke the silence. "How come a man of your training is out of a job?"

It sounded like the beginning of an inquiry. Since his name was not involved, Hedrock replied quickly, "I've been wasting my time out on the planets. Damn fool!"

Greer seemed to consider that, for several minutes went by. At last he said, "What brought you back?"

There could be no hesitating over that. If Greer went "upstairs", and examined his clothes, he'd find the name of Daniel Neelan written in a notebook. It was a possibility that had to be taken into account. "My brother's death," Hedrock said.

"Oh, your brother died?"

"Yes." It was the story he had originally intended to tell. Now, he could tell it without naming names. "Yes, he used to send me an allowance. When that stopped, I made inquiries, and it seems he's been missing for a year, unregistered. It'll take about six months more to close the estate, but, as you probably know, the courts recognize non-registration as proof of death in these days of multiple assassinations."

"I know," was all Greer said.

In the silence that followed, Hedrock thought, "Let him mull that over." It wouldn't do any harm, in the event he did find the notation about Neelan, for Greer to believe that Gil and Dan Neelan had no strong feelings for each other. "It's more than ten years," Hedrock said aloud, "since I saw him. I found I didn't have the faintest sense of kinship. I didn't give a damn whether he was dead or alive. Funny."

Greer said, "You're going back into space?"

Hedrock shook his head. "Nope. Earth for me from now on. There's more excitement, fun, pleasure."

"I wouldn't," said Greer, after a silence, "exchange my last year in space for all the pleasure in Imperial City."

"Each to his own taste—" Hedrock began.

And stopped. His will—to get the man up to the insulation room—collapsed to secondary importance. For here was information. The astonishing thing was that he hadn't guessed it before. It had been implicit in every facet of this affair. "My last year in space—" Why, of course. Kershaw, Gil Neelan, Greer and other men had taken this ship on a trial interstellar cruise. They had been to one of the near stars, possibly Alpha Centauri, or Sirius or Procyon—in spite of all his years of life, Hedrock trembled with excitement as he ran over the names of the famous nearby star systems.

Slowly, the emotional repercussions of Greer's words died out of him. The picture of what had happened was far from clear, except for one thing. Greer had volunteered the new fact. He wanted to talk. He could be led into saying more. Hedrock said, "My idea of life isn't cruising around space looking for meteors. I've done it, and I know."

"Meteors!" Greer exploded. "Are you crazy? Do you think the Empress of Isher would be interested in meteors? This is a hundred-billion credit deal. Do you hear that? And she's going to pay it, too."

He began to pace the floor, obviously stimulated. He whirled suddenly on Hedrock, "Do you know where I've been?" he demanded. "I—"

He stopped. The muscles of his face worked convulsively. Finally, he managed a grim smile. "Oh, no, you don't," he said. "You're not pulling anything out of me. Not that it really matters, but—" He stood there and stared at Hedrock. Abruptly, he twisted on his heel, climbed the stairway, and disappeared from view.

Hedrock gazed at the stairway, conscious that the time had come for action. He examined the ceiling metal with a modified transparency, and nodded finally in satisfaction. Four inches thick, the usual alloy of lead and "heavy" beryllium, atomically processed. The transparency also showed the exact spot where Greer was sitting, a blurred figure, reading a book. Or rather, holding a book. It was impossible to see whether he was reading.

Hedrock felt himself cold, grim. His only emotion was a remote, deadly pleasure that Greer was sitting up there, smugly imagining himself in control of the situation.

He maneuvered the heavy polisher directly under the spot where Greer was sitting, and turned its finely toothed surface to point upward. Then he began his estimation. Greer had looked about one hundred and seventy pounds. Two thirds of that, roughly, was one hundred and fourteen. To be on the safe

56

side, allow for a blow that would kill a man of a hundred pounds. Greer didn't look too physically fit. He'd need the handicap.

There was, of course, the four-inch floor to figure in. Fortunately, its resistance was a formula based on tension. He made the necessary adjustments, and then pressed the button control.

Greer crumpled. Hedrock went upstairs to where the man lay sprawled on a leg-rest chair. He examined the unconscious body with a color transparency, for detail. No bones broken. And the heart still beat. Good. A dead man wouldn't be able to answer questions. There were a lot of questions.

It required considerable mathematical work to plot a system of force lines that would bind Greer into a reasonably comfortable position, allowing his arms and legs to move, and his body to turn, and yet be capable of holding him forever if necessary.

7

HEDROCK SPENT THE NEXT HALF HOUR GOING OVER THE ship. There were many locked doors and packed storerooms which he temporarily by-passed. He wanted a general idea of what the inside looked like, and he wanted it quickly.

What he found in that cursory search did not satisfy him. He had a spaceship that couldn't leave its hangar; a ship, moreover, which it would be dangerous for him to leave now that he had control of it.

It might be guarded. The fact that he had not seen any of Innelda's soldiers proved nothing. They could be wearing invisibility suits. The Empress would be desperately anxious not to draw the attention of Weapon Shop observers to concentrations of government forces. And so, Robert Hedrock had come along an apparently deserted street, and entered the ship of ships before the commander of the protecting forces could make up his mind to stop him.

If that picture was even close to the reality, then it would be virtually impossible for him to get away from the machine without being picked up for questioning. It was a risk he dared not take. Which left him where? He went thoughtfully down to the insulation room, and found Greer conscious. The man glared at him with mingled hate and fear.

"You don't think you're going to get away with this," he said in a voice that trembled. "When the Empress finds out about this, she'll—"

Hedrock cut him off. "Where are the others?" he asked. "Where are Kershaw and—" He hesitated—"my brother, Gil?"

The brown eyes that had been glaring at him widened. Greer shuddered visibly, then he said, "Go to hell!" But he sounded frightened.

Hedrock went on in a steady voice, "If I were you I'd start worrying about what would happen to you if I should decide to turn you over to the Empress."

Greer's face acquired a bleached look. He swallowed hard, and then said huskily, "Don't be a fool! There's enough here for both of us. We can both cash in—but we've got to be careful—She's got the ship surrounded. I figured they'd let somebody through, but that's why I greeted you with that ninety thousand cycle cannon—just in case they tried to come in, too."

Hedrock said, "What about the telestat? Is it possible to make calls outside?"

"Just through the 'stat in the Trellis Minor Building."

"Oh!" said Hedrock, and bit his lip in vexation. For once he had over-reached himself. It had seemed logical to render that particular 'stat useless, and so head off all other candidates for the job that was being offered. Then he hadn't expected that the trail would lead directly to the interstellar ship itself.

"What do you get on any other 'stat?"

"A fellow named Zeydel," said Greer in a grim tone.

It required several seconds for Hedrock to recall where he had heard that name before. At the Empress' table, some months earlier. One of the men had expressed abhorrence at the idea that Innelda would employ such a creature. Hedrock remembered her answer. "God made rats," she had said, "and God made Zeydel. My scientists have found a use for rats in their laboratories, and I have found a use for Zeydel. Does that answer your question, sir?" She had finished haughtily.

The man who had brought up the subject was known for his sharp tongue. He had flashed back at her, "I see. You have human beings in your laboratories who experiment on rats, and now you have found a rat to experiment on human beings."

The remark had brought a flush to Innelda's cheeks, and for the man two weeks banishment from her table. But it was apparent that she still had a use for Zeydel. Which was unfortunate, because it seemed to preclude bribery, that important adjunct of recent Isher civilization. Hedrock did not

58

accept the defeat as final. He loaded Greer, force lines and all, on to an antigravity plate, and carted him upstairs to one of the bedrooms in the upper half of the ship. And then he started on his second exploration of the ship. This time, though every minute now seemed valuable—and a crisis imminent—it was no cursory search.

He went through every room, using a power drill to break recalcitrant locks. The personal quarters above the control room held him longest. But Greer had been there before him. Nothing remained that gave any clue to the real owner's whereabouts. Greer must have had plenty of time to destroy the evidence, and he had used it well. There were no letters, no personal property, nothing that would ever cause embarrassment to a murderer. It was in the nose of the ship, in an airlock, that Hedrock made his prize find. A fully equipped lifeboat, powered by two replicas of the giant engines in the main machine, was snugly fitted there into a formfitting cradle. The little boat—little only by comparison; it was nearly a hundred feet long—seemed to be in perfect condition and ready to fly.

Hedrock examined the controls carefully, and noticed with excitement that, beside the normal accelerator, was a gleaming white lever, with the letters INFINITY DRIVE printed on it. Its presence seemed to indicate that even the lifeboat had the interstellar drive mechanism built into it. Theoretically, he could sit down at the controls, launch the lifeboat into the air, and escape into space at a speed which pursuing ships would not be able to match. He examined the launching devices. They were automatic, he discovered. The spaceboat need merely glide forward from its cradle under normal drive, and its movement would activate the electrically operated lock. At tremendous speed, the lock-door would slide open; the boat would race through it. And the airlock would close the moment it was clear.

No doubt about it. He could now make his escape. Hedrock climbed out of the lifeboat, and went down to the main control room at the ground level. He felt undecided. Within a few hours of escaping from the Imperial palace, he had captured the interstellar ship. He had succeeded, accordingly, where the forces of the Empress and of the Weapon Makers had failed. It was time now to be more careful, and that brought up a number of problems, all interrelated. How could he turn the big ship over to the Weapon Makers without endangering himself, and without starting a battle between the navies of the government and of the Weapon Makers? The decisive factor was that the latter wouldn't receive his note, giving this address, until noon the following day.

Under normal circumstances, the interval would probably pass without incident. But unfortunately a stranger had been observed going aboard. When Zeydel reported that to Innelda, she'd become suspicious. She might give Greer a little while to get in touch with her agents, and explain the event. But she wouldn't wait very long. Perhaps already she had made several attempts to contact Greer. Hedrock seated himself in the control chair, watched the main 'stat for activity. And considered his situation.

After five and three quarter minutes there was a click, a call light began to blink, and a siren gave off a low musical hum. The activity continued for two minutes, and then ceased. Hedrock waited. At the end of thirteen minutes, there was a click again, and the process repeated. So that was the pattern. Zeydel must have been instructed to "call Greer every fifteen minutes." Presumably, if he failed to answer, further action would be taken.

Hedrock went down to the engine room and set to work refitting a motor. It seemed unlikely that he would have time to put together the two engines that would be needed to enable the big ship to fly, but it was worth making the attempt. At first he went up to the control room every hour to see if the call was still coming through. But finally he rigged up a 'stat in the engine room, and connected it to the one in the control room. From then on, he could follow the calls without ceasing work.

What Innelda would do when she ran out of patience was a matter of conjecture. But Hedrock could imagine her having already mobilized the fleet, with the hope that, if the interstellar ship tried to get away, the mighty guns of the battleships would knock it out of the sky before it could gather speed.

It was that possibility that made it dangerous for him to risk an escape in the lifeboat. If it were brought down, that would end man's hope of reaching the stars. His plan must be to hold off the Empress' forces until a *number* of possibilities existed for success. And then, and not till then, make an all out effort to gain an unqualified victory for himself and the Shops. He couldn't expect to do anything until twelve noon tomorrow.

At six o'clock, eighteen hours before the deadline, the 'stat failed to call out. Fifteen minutes later, it was again silent. Hedrock hurried to the galley, had a bite to eat, and carried sandwiches and coffee to Greer. He removed one of the force lines, so that Greer could move one arm freely enough to feed himself. At six-twenty-nine Hedrock settled himself at the control board. Once more, the 'stat failed to show any activity. Either a further step would now be taken, or else

Innelda was giving up for the night. It was a choice Hedrock dared not leave to chance. He switched on his end of the telestat, the voice connection only—the vision plate remained dark—and dialed the nearest police station. He intended to pretend that he knew nothing about what was going on, and it was interesting therefore that they let him dial the whole number. It was particularly interesting because he wanted them to believe that he was making an unsuspecting call to the police.

The familiar click was his first knowledge that he had made a connection. Before the person at the other end could say anything, Hedrock whispered loudly, "Is that the police department? I'm a prisoner aboard what seems to be a spaceship, and I want to be rescued."

There was a long pause, and then a man said in a low voice, "What address are you at?"

Hedrock gave it, and went on succinctly to explain that he had been hired to repair some atomic motors, but was now forcibly being detained by a man named Rel Greer. His account was interrupted, "Where's Greer now?"

"He's lying down in his cabin upstairs,"

"Just a moment," said the man.

There was a pause, and the unmistakable voice of the Empress Innelda said, "What is your name?"

"Daniel Neelan," said Hedrock. He added urgently, "But please hurry. Greer may come down at any minute. I don't want to be caught here."

"Why don't you just open the doors and walk out?"

Hedrock had his answer for that, also. He explained that Greer had removed from the control board the devices for opening and shutting the doors. "He has them up in his room," he finished.

"I see." There was a momentary silence. He could imagine her swift mind visualizing the situation and its possibilities. She must have been in the process of making up her mind, for she said almost immediately, "Mr. Neelan, your call to the police station has been switched to the offices of the government secret service. The reason is that quite unwittingly you have walked in upon a situation in which the government is interested." She added quickly, "Do not be alarmed."

Hedrock decided to say nothing.

Innelda continued swiftly, "Mr. Neelan, can you turn on the vision plate? It is important that you see the person to whom you are talking."

"I can turn it on, so that I could see you, but the section of the 'stat which would enable you to see me has been removed."

Her reply was acid toned. "We are familiar with Greer's

secretiveness about his personal appearance." She broke off. "But quick now, I want you to have a look at me."

Hedrock switched on the plate, and watched while the image of the Empress of Isher grew on to it. He hesitated for a few moments, and then whispered, "Your Majesty!"

"You recognize me?"

"Yes, yes, but—"

She cut him off. "Mr. Neelan, you occupy a unique position in the world of great affairs. Your government, your— Empress—require your loyal and faithful services."

Hedrock said, "Your Majesty, forgive me, but please hurry."

"I must make myself clear; you must understand. This afternoon, Dan Neelan, when I was informed that a strange young man—that is, yourself—had entered the Greer spaceship, I immediately ordered the execution of a Captain Hedrock, a Weapon Shop spy, whom I had previously tolerated in the palace."

She was mixing her times a little, it seemed to Hedrock, and also mixing truth with falsehood. But it was not up to him to correct her. What did interest him was her refusal to be hurried. He had an idea that she regarded this as an unexpected opportunity, but that she would not worry too much about what happened to Daniel Neelan. She must take it for granted that she could always go back to bargaining with Greer, and she was probably right. She went on, her face intent, her voice low but firm: "I tell you this to illustrate graphically the completeness and extent of the precautions I am prepared to take to insure that my will shall prevail. Consider Captain Hedrock's fate as symbolical of what will befall anyone who dares to oppose me in this matter, or who bungles his part of the job. Here is what you must and will do. As of this moment you are a soldier in the government service. You will continue to pretend to repair the drive motors of the ship, and actually you will do enough work to convince Greer that you are fulfilling your obligations to him. But every spare moment that you have you will spend in taking apart those motors which can still operate. I am assured that it is possible to do this so skilfully that only an expert would notice that anything was wrong.

"Now, please listen carefully. As soon as you have paralysed the motive power of the ship, you must take the first opportunity to advise us. A single word will do. You can switch on your 'stat, and say, 'Now', 'Ready' or anything like that, and we will break in. We have eight one-hundred-million cycle guns in position. That is the plan. So it shall be. Within twenty-four hours of its successful conclusion, you will receive a tremendous reward for your assistance."

Her intense voice died away. Her tensed body relaxed. The flame died from her gaze. There was suddenly a warm and generous smile around her eyes and lips. She said in a quiet voice, "I hope, Dan Neelan, I have made myself clear."

There was no doubt of that. In spite of himself, in spite of his previous association with her, Hedrock was fascinated. He had made no mistake in believing that Imperial Innelda would play a foremost role in every crisis of this unsettled age.

His mind began to consider the implications of what she had said; and he was shocked. The Empress' voice interrupted his thoughts:

"—Zeydel, take over!"

The face, head and shoulders of a man of about forty-five replaced her image on the plate. Zeydel had slate-colored eyes, a thin beak of a nose, and lips that formed a long slit across his face. There was a faint, grim smile on his raffish countenance, but his voice had a flat quality as he said:

"You have heard our glorious ruler's commands. This scoundrel Greer has deliberately set himself against the crown. He has an invention which endangers the State, and which must be completely withheld from the knowledge of the public.

"Accordingly—and listen well—if it should prove necessary, or if the opportunity occurs, you are herewith given permission to kill Greer as an enemy of the State, in the name of her Imperial Majesty, Innelda. And now, before I break off, are there any questions?"

They were taking his cooperation for granted. He realized that he was expected to make an answer. "No questions," he whispered. "I am a loyal subject of her Majesty. I understand everything."

"Good. If we don't hear from you by eleven tomorrow, we will attack anyway. May you prove worthy of the Empress' trust."

There was a click. Hedrock broke the connection at his own end, and went down to the engine room again. He was disturbed at the time limitation that had been set. But it seemed to him that he ought to be able to delay the assault for an hour or even more.

He took an anti-sleep pill, and set to work on the motors. Shorly after midnight he completed the balancing adjustments on one of the drives, and so had half the power that was necessary to lift a ship as large as this one into the air.

All too swiftly the hours went by. At ten after nine, Hedrock realized suddenly how much time had passed. He estimated, then, that he was a good two hours away from readying the second motor, and that, for that reason alone, some kind of delay was in order. He fed Greer, ate a hurried breakfast, and then worked on the motor until twenty minutes to eleven.

At that time, perspiring from his efforts, his job still not completed, he switched on the 'stat connection and called Zeydel. The man's face image appeared on the plate almost instantly; he was like a fox in his eagerness. His eyes flashed, his mouth trembled. "Yes?" he breathed.

"No," said Hedrock. He spoke swiftly, "Greer has just now gone up to the control room. He's been with me all morning, so I'm only now in a position to start putting the motors out of commission. It'll take till twelve-thirty, or one. Make it one to be absolutely sure. I—"

Zeydel's image faded from the screen, and that of the Empress Innelda replaced it. Her green eyes were narrowed the faintest bit, but her voice was calm as she said, "We accept the delay, but only till twelve. Get busy—and leave the 'stat on; not the vision plate, of course, just the voice—*and have those drives paralysed in time!*"

"I'll try, your Majesty," Hedrock whispered.

He had gained another hour.

He went back to his delicate task of adjusting an atomic motor back into working condition. He caught glimpses of his perspiring face in the gleaming metal of the tools he used. He felt himself tense, and no longer sure that the work he was doing would serve any useful purpose. In the sky above the great city, the government fleet would be out in force. And the chances of a last minute action by the Weapon Makers seemed more remote every passing instant. He pictured the noon delivery at the Meteor corporation. His letter to Peter Cadron, giving this address would be passed on swiftly—but Cadron might be in conference; he might have stepped through a transmitter to the other side of the earth; he might be at lunch. Besides, people didn't open their mail as if their lives depended on it. Accordingly, the possibility was strong that it would be one, or even two o'clock before the Weapon Shop councilor read the letter from Robert Hedrock.

It was eleven-thirty when the straining Hedrock realized that the second motor would not be ready in time. He continued working, because the sounds would convince the Empress that he was obeying instructions. But he realized it was time to make decisions. He'd have to get up to the lifeboat, of course. Whatever else went wrong or right, it represented his personal hope of escape. And since it also included the interstellar drive it was by itself as valuable as the larger ship. If it got away, then man would reach the stars. If it didn't, if it was brought down, then—but there was no point in considering failure.

But how could he get up to the lifeboat while the 'stat was on? If he should cease his noisy activity, she and Zeydel would immediately become suspicious. It would take him, he estimated, five minutes to climb to the lifeboat. Considering everything, that was a long time. So long, in fact, that a further effort to confuse Innelda was justified. Hedrock hesitated, and then approached the 'stat.

"Your Majesty," he said in a loud whisper.

"Yes?"

The reply was so prompt that he had a sudden vision of her sitting before a bank of telestats, keeping in touch with all the facets of this enterprise. He said quickly: "Your Majesty, it will be impossible for me to put all the motors out of commission by the time you have set me. There are seventeen drive engines down here, and I have only had time to work on nine of them. Do you mind if I make a suggestion?"

"Go ahead." Her tone was non-committal.

"My idea is that I go upstairs and try to overpower Greer. I might possibly catch him by surprise."

"Yes." There was an odd note in her voice. "Yes, you might." She hesitated, then she continued firmly, "I may as will tell you, Neelan, that we are becoming suspicious of you."

"I don't understand, your Majesty."

She seemed not to hear. "We have been trying since early yesterday afternoon to contact Greer. In the past he has always responded within an hour or so, and it is unusual, to say the least, that he has not even deigned to answer our attempts at communication. For all he knows we are prepared to meet his exorbitant terms and every one of his absurd conditions."

"I still don't see—"

"Let me put it like this," she said coolly. "At this final hour we do not take chances. You have permission to go upstairs and overpower Greer. In fact, I order you to take the risks of a soldier and prevent him from successfully launching this ship out of its hangar. However, just in case our vague suspicions of you have any basis, I am now, *this instant,* ordering the attack. If you have any private plans of your own, abandon them now, and cooperate with us. Climb up, while the attack is in progress, and do anything that is necessary against Greer. But you'll have to hurry."

Her voice grew stronger, and it was clear that she was giving orders into other 'stats, as she cried in a tone that was like a deep violin note, "All forces act. Break in!"

Hedrock heard that command as he started for the stairway. He had to pause to open the radiation door, and then he was racing up the steps, still hopeful, still convinced that in spite of what had happened he could climb up above the ground level before anybody could stop him.

The first shot struck then. It shook the ship. It was violent beyond his wildest preconception. It brought a moment of horrible daze, and the mind-racking thought that he had forgotten concussion. He raced on up, up, the fear of defeat already in his heart. The second titanic shot sent him reeling back. But he recovered and climbed on.

The third shot raged then. And blood spurted from his nose; a warm stream trickled out of his ears. The fourth shot—he was dimly aware that he was half-way to the control room—crumpled him in a heap. He half-rolled down an entire section of the stairway. And the fifth shot caught him as he was staggering erect.

He knew his defeat now, a sick and deadly knowledge, but he kept moving his legs, and felt amazed when he reached the next level. The sixth intolerable explosion caught him there at the head of that long stairway, and sent him spinning down like a leaf engulfed in a storm. There was a door at the bottom; and he closed it with automatic intention. He stared dully as the great door lifted from its hinges, grazed him as it fell, and clanged to the floor. That was the seventh shot.

Like an animal now, he retreated from pain, down the next line of steps, instinctively locking the lower door. He was standing there, infinitely weary, half leaning against the wall when the shouts of men roused his stunned mind. Voices, he thought then, inside the ship. He shook his head, unbelievingly. The voices came nearer; and then abruptly, the truth penetrated.

They were in. It had only taken seven shots.

A man shouted arrogantly from the other side of the door beside which he was standing, "Quick, break it down! Capture everybody aboard. That's orders!"

8

HEDROCK BEGAN TO RETREAT. IT WAS A SLOW BUSINESS, because his mind wouldn't gather around any one thought, and his reflexes were disorganized.

His knees trembled as he kept going down the stairs. Down, down—the feeling came that he was climbing down into his grave. Not, he thought, that there was much farther to go now. The storerooms were past. Next would be the insulation room, then the repair room, then the engine room, then the drive chamber; and then—

And then—

Hope came. Because there was a way. The ship was lost, of course. And with it the chance of all the billions of human beings who might have carried the torch of civilization to the farthest stars of the universe—their chance, their destiny, their hope of greater happiness was gone. But once more there was hope for him. He reached the engine room, and forgot all else but the work that had to be done. It took a precious minute to discover which of the electric switches controlled the ship's lighting system and other power functions. During that minute the floors shuddered as another of the doors he had locked went down with a distant clang before the hissing roar of a mobile unit. Instantly, the shouting of men came nearer.

Hedrock began to pull switches. He wanted all the upper lights off. It should take them several minutes to get more. He had already visually located the six-foot drill he wanted. He floated it out on its antigravity base, pushing it urgently down the two flights of stairs from the repair room, where it had been, down past the engine room, into the great drive chamber that was the final room of the big spaceship. And there, in spite of himself, in spite of urgency, Hedrock paused and stared at what must be the stellar drive itself.

Here was the treasure that all the fighting was about. Yesterday—how long ago that seemed—he hadn't had time to come down to this room. Now, he had to make the time. He snatched the transparency bar of the giant drill and focused its penetrating light at the thirty-foot-thick drive shaft. He saw dark mist—and realized his failure. The metal was too hard, too thick. There were too many interlayers and reflectors. No known transparency would ever approach the core of that drive.

Defeated, he whirled and began to run, pushing the drill which, weightless though it was, nevertheless offered a "mass" resistance to his straining muscles. He got through the first door of the bottom lock, then the second, then the third, and then he stood there in a wild surmise. He had been gathering his reserves of strength and will for the job of drilling a six-foot hole through the earth on a steep slanting thrust for the surface. He didn't have to. The hole, the passageway, was there. A line of dim ceiling lights made a straight but upward slanting path into the distance.

It was not the moment to think of why it was there. Hedrock

grabbed the transparency bar, squeezed past the now un-necessary drill, and raced along the tunnel. It was much longer than he would have had time to drill. The angle of ascent was only about twenty degrees. But actually the greater distance was all to the good. The farther he got away from the ship before emerging into the open, the better.

He reached the end suddenly. It was a metal door; and, using the transparency, he could see that beyond it was an empty cellar. The door had a simple latch that opened at his touch and closed behind him like amorphous metal sinking tracelessly into a solid wall. Hedrock paused inside the cellar and studied the door. He had taken it for granted that Greer had been back from Centaurus for a long time. But there was another explanation. Not Greer, but Kershaw and the others, had built this. They, too, had been cautious about their con-tacts with the outside world. It was possible that Greer had not even known of this passageway. In fact—Hedrock felt suddenly positive—the man would never have left him alone in the engine room yesterday morning, so near an exit, if he had known. The other, the telestat contacts with the outside world had probably been handed into Greer's control as gen-eral handy man by those brilliant nitwits, Kershaw and Gil Neelan, who thought of every precaution against outside interference but had failed to protect themselves against their own employee.

It was an interesting but academic point in view of what had happened. Depressed, Hedrock headed for a set of stairs to his left. Halfway up, the stairs branched. The left way led up to a rather ornate door beyond which his transparency showed a vacant kitchen. The right way proved to be the one he wanted.

Hedrock laid the transparency down on the steps. He wouldn't be needing it any more. He straightened, opened the second door, and stepped into bright sunlight. He found him-self in the back yard of a large, vacant house. There was the usual green wonder of lawn, the perpetually flowering gar-den, the carplane garage, and a high fence with a gate. The gate opened easily from inside on to a back-alley boulevard, the kind where the sidewalks hug the sides of the street. Far-ther along, Hedrock could see a broad thoroughfare.

He hurried toward it, anxious to identify it so that he could judge how far he was from the spaceship. Knowing where he was would give him a better idea of what he must do, *could* do, next.

There was a uniformed guard at the corner, and he wore the glittering viewer headpiece. He waved at Hedrock from a distance.

"How're things going?"

"We're in!" Hedrock called. "Keep your eyes peeled."

"Don't worry. There's a solid line of us out here."

Hedrock turned away, thoughtfully, and walked hastily back the way he had come. Trapped. The streets would be covered for blocks; and, in minutes, a yelling crew would smash the last of the hard doors that barred their way in the spaceship, realize what had happened, and the search with its certainty of capture would be on. Or, worse still, perhaps they were already by the final barrier, and in minutes would break from the house, where the tunnel ended, and seeing him, swoop for the kill.

He vaulted a high fence into another back yard. There was a line of viewer-helmeted men along the front of the house. But now that he was heading for the ship, with the hope it suddenly offered, the spirit of retreat faded. Nobody tried to stop him. And, after a tense minute, he had to smile at the psychology that permitted a man to head toward a center of infection, but not away from it. He crossed boldly to the corner of the street, from where he could see the needle-shaped hangar just down the block. A few seconds later he reached the ship. No one tried to stop him as he climbed gingerly through the jagged gap the cannon had made, and so into the control room.

The lights he had turned off were on. That was the first thing Hedrock noticed. The searchers had reached the engine room. Presently, they would come surging up to explore the rest of the ship. Meanwhile, he had the opportunity he needed. Hedrock glanced around the control room. There were several dozen men standing around, and every one of them was dressed in the regulation insulation suit. There was no suspicion in their eyes.

To them he was just one more member of the secret police, wearing protective clothing in a radioactive area.

Crash! The sound coming from deep in the ship galvanized Hedrock. *That must be the door to the drive chamber*. His freedom was just now being discovered. In seconds, the alarm would clamor forth. Hedrock walked without haste toward the stairway, jostled past several men waiting there, and began to climb up. It was as simple as that. He came to the lifeboat. He searched it quickly. It was untenanted. With a sigh, he sank into the multipurpose chair before the control board, drew a shaky breath, and pressed the launching lever.

Like a ball rolling down a glass incline, the little ship slid up into the air.

The old and wonderful city, seen from the height of half a mile, sparkled in the sun. It seemed very close, some of the spearheads of buildings almost scraping the bottom of his ship as he flew. Hedrock sat almost without thought. His first wonder that the warships had not attacked him had already yielded to the belief that they were on the lookout for an eight-hundred-foot spaceship; this tiny craft resembled at a distance a public carplane, or a dozen types of pleasure craft. He had two purposes. The first one was to escape, if he could, to one of his hiding places. Failing that he intended to use the special drive of the lifeboat to help him get away.

It was a dark spot on the upper rim of the rear-view 'stat that brought him out of his hopeful mood. The spot hurtled down out of the blue, became a ship, became a thousand-foot cruiser. Simultaneously, his general call 'stat (usable now that he was out in the open) broke into life. A stern voice said:

"Didn't you hear the universal order to ground? Carry on straight ahead, stay on your present level till you come to the military airport beacon due east. Land there, or be blown to bits."

Hedrock's fingers, reaching for the white accelerator, paused in midair. The command showed no suspicion of his identity. His gaze flashed to the telestat plates again and saw that, except for the cruiser, he was alone in the air. All traffic *had* been forced down.

Hedrock flashed a frowning glance at the cruiser on the 'stat plate. It showed directly above him and startlingly close. Too close. His eyes narrowed. It blocked an entire section of the upper sky from him. He realized the truth as a second cruiser slipped down to his right, and a third cruiser slid to his left, and a small swarm of destroyers rocketed into view behind and in front of him. The first ship, in almost hugging him, had screened the approach of the others. And there was no doubt that, whatever the army might be, the fleet was efficient. A second time his hand reached toward the white accelerator. He clenched it, and then paused as the long, patrician face of the Empress appeared on the general call plate.

"Neelan," she said, "I don't understand. Surely, you're not going to be foolish enough to oppose your government."

Hedrock made no reply. He was tilting his ship ever so slightly. He had his eye on an open space above and between the destroyers ahead. And, besides, his end of these conversations could no longer be carried on in whispers. Which meant that he would have to disguise his voice, something which he hadn't done for years. It was not the moment to risk his future relationship with her by an unskilful performance.

"Dan Neelan—" The Empress' voice was low and intense— "think before you commit yourself irrevocably to ruin. My

70

offer is still open. Simply land that lifeboat as directed and—"

Her voice went on, but Hedrock was intent on escape. Her interruption had given him time to make a further adjustment on his course, and his little ship was titled now toward the southern hemisphere in the general direction of Centaurus. It was a rough aim, but he had a suspicion that the acceleration he'd need to escape the warships would black him out for a while and he might as well be going somewhere that he knew about.

"—I offer you one billion credits—"

His fingers were clenched around the white lever on which were engraved the words, INFINITY DRIVE, and now that the time had come he did not hesitate. With a flick of his arm, he pulled the lever all the way over.

There was a blow as from a sledge hammer.

9

THE MORNING DRAGGED. THE EMPRESS PACED THE FLOOR of her office in front of the mirrors that lined the walls, a tall, handsome young woman.

She thought once, "How strained I look, like an overworked kitchen maid. I'm beginning to feel sorry for myself and all the hard things I have to do. I'm getting old."

She felt older. For the dozenth time, she turned on one of the bank of telestats and stared at the men working in the drive chamber of the Greer spaceship. She had a frantic sense of wanting to shout at them, to urge them to hurry, *hurry*. Didn't they realize that any hour, any minute, the Weapon Shops might discover where the ship was hidden, and attack with all their power?

A score of times during that long morning, she thought, "Destroy the ship now, before it's too late."

With a nervous flick of her finger, she turned on her news 'stat and listened to the clamor that roared at her: *Weapon Shops charge that the Empress has secret of interstellar travel. . . . Weapon Shops demand that the Empress release to the people the secret of—*

She clicked it off, and stood briefly startled by the sharp silence. After a moment she felt better. They *didn't* know. That was the essence of the reports. The Weapon Shops didn't know the secret. It was true that they had somehow divined what she had. But too late. As soon as the ship was destroyed—

71

she felt another flare of anxiety—there would remain the one doubtful point, one man, the incomprehensible Dan Neelan.

But Neelan must be dead, or lost. During the two seconds that his little ship had been within range of the warship radar beams, technical officers had estimated its acceleration at well beyond that which a human being could endure and remain conscious. The pressure that had produced the unconscious state would continue for an indefinite period. Let the Weapon Shops rave and rant. The House of Isher had survived greater storms than this.

An involuntary glance at the 'stat, which was attuned to the Greer spaceship, jarred her mind back to her basic danger. For a long minute she stared at the uncompleted work. Then, trembling, she broke the connection. It was a nightmare, she thought, this waiting.

It was heartening to listen to the early-afternoon news. It was more reassuring. Everything about the Weapon Shops was against them. She mustered a wry smile. How low she had sunk when her own propaganda could cheer her up.

But it did. So much so that her nerves quieted sufficiently for her to feel up to an interview she had been putting off all morning. The interview with Greer. She sat cold as rock while the frightened wretch poured out his story. The man was almost beside himself with terror, and his tongue kept running off into pleas for mercy. For a time that didn't bother her. There was only the thread of his tale about Kershaw and Neelan and—

And Neelan!

She sighed her understanding. What an impregnable wall of purpose she had smashed up against. The relationship, it seemed to her, explained the unexpected resistance he had offered her, though there was still no explanation of how he had located the ship. Whatever the details, within a few hours of boarding the machine he had had control of it. His efforts to get the drives working again had been herculean, but the odds against his success had been out of proportion to the enormousness of the task. That was particularly true, and even unfair, because in the final issue she herself had ordered the attack on the basis of her terrible anxiety. Logically, she should have accepted his reasons for delaying the assault. There was no question but that she had run up against a remarkable man.

She came out of her reverie, and said softly to Greer, "And where did you leave Kershaw and the others?"

The man broke into a frenzy of babbling, something about there being seven habitable planets altogether in the Alpha Centauri system, three of them lovelier than earth—"And I swear I left them on one of those. They'll be all right. The first ship will pick them up. All I wanted was to get back here and sell the invention. It's a crime, of course. But these days everybody's out for himself."

She knew he was lying about where he had left the men. She felt cold and merciless. People who were afraid always did that to her. She had a sense of loathing, as if something unclean was near her. It didn't really matter whether such people lived or died. She hesitated in spite of the simple logic, and the simpler impulse involved. It took a long second to realize why. It was because, fantastically, she was afraid, too. Not in the way he was. Not for herself. But for the House of Isher.

She stiffened. "Take him back to his cell," she said. "I shall decide later what to do with him."

But she knew that she was going to let him live. Contempt burned in her at the weakness. She was become one with the mobs that raged through the streets shouting for the secrets of the interstellar drive.

Her personal 'stat buzzed. She clicked it on; and her eyes widened as she saw that it was Admiral Dirn.

"Yes," she managed to say finally, "yes, I'll be right over."

She climbed to her feet with an unnatural sense of urgency. The spaceship was ready, waiting now for her to drain its secret. But in an affair like this, with the mighty Weapon Makers opposing her, one minute could be too late. She ran for the door.

The Greer spaceship—she continued to call it that irritably for want of a better name—seemed a tiny thing in that vast military hangar. But as her carplane with its attendant patrol vessels flew nearer, it began to take on size. It towered above her finally, a long, mottled-metal, cigar-shaped structure lying horizontally on the cradle in which it was berthed. It didn't take long to walk the four hundred feet through door after shattered door. Her eyes studied the gigantic drive shaft. She saw that the plates had been loosened but not removed. And after a moment she looked questioningly at the uniformed officer who stood a respectful distance behind her. The man bowed.

"As you see, Your Majesty, your orders have been carried out to the letter. Nothing inside the drive has been touched or seen, and the workmen who disconnected the plates are the ones who were chosen by you personally from case histories submitted this morning. Not one has sufficient knowledge of science to analyse even an ordinary drive let alone a special type."

"Good."

She turned and saw that a troop of men was coming in. They all saluted.

73

The men, she saw, had their orders. They began to remove the loosened plates with a quiet efficiency. In two hours, the job was done. The secret of the drive was carefully integrated into her brain. She stood finally behind a ray shield watching an energy gun dissolve the drive core into a mass of sagging, then molten metal. Her patience had no end. She waited until there was a splotchy mound of white-hot metal on the floor; and then, satisfied at last, climbed into her carplane.

Dark clouds rode the late afternoon sky as she returned to the palace.

10

IT WASN'T THAT THE DARKNESS LIGHTENED. HEDROCK SAGGED for a long time with his eyes open.

Slowly, he grew aware of a quietness around him, a lack of pressure, of movement. The elements of his mind gathered a little closer together. He straightened in the control chair, and glanced at the 'stat plates. He was staring into space. In every direction were stars. No sun, nothing but needlesharp points of light varying in brilliance. And no pressure of acceleration, no gravity. It wasn't an unusual experience; but this time it was different. He glanced at the Infinity Drive, and it was still in gear. That was the trouble. It was in gear. The speedometer showed impossible figures; the automatic calendar said that the time was 7 P.M., August 28, 4791 Isher. Hedrock nodded to himself. So he had been unconscious for twenty-two days; and during that time the ship had gone—he glanced at the speedometer, it was registering something over four hundred million miles a second. At that rate, he was covering the distance between Earth and Centaurus every eighteen hours. The problem was to retrace his course.

Thoughtfully, he eased the clutch of the automatic half-circle into the steering shaft. It whirred and then went *ticaticatac* a hundred and eighty times, very fast. The stars reeled, but settled into steadiness as the stop watch showed three seconds. A perfect hairpin turn in twelve hundred million miles. At that rate he would be within sight of Earth's sun in another twenty-two days. No, wait! It wasn't as simple as that. He couldn't subject himself again to the kind of pressure that had held him unconscious so long. After some estimations, he set the drive lever at three quarters reverse. And waited. The

74

question was, how soon had he recovered consciousness after the pressure stopped? Two hours passed, and still nothing had happened. His head kept drooping, his eyes closing. But the blow of deceleration didn't come.

Uneasily expectant, Hedrock finally went to sleep on one of the couches.

There was a jar that shook his bones. Hedrock awakened with a start, but he calmed swiftly as he felt the steady pressure on his body. It was strong, like the current of a very heavy wind. But now that he had taken the first shock, it was bearable. He ached to leap up and examine the speedometer. But he held himself where he was. He was acutely conscious of the tingling readjustments going on in his body, the electronic, atomic, molecular, neural, muscular readjustments. He gave himself thirty minutes before moving. Then he headed for the control boards and peered into the 'stats. But there was nothing to see. The calendar said August 29th, 11:03 P.M., and the speedometer was down to three hundred and fifty million miles. At his present deceleration, the lifeboat should come to a full stop in about thirty-two days, at most.

The third day also showed a reduction of more than eleven million miles a second. The hollow feeling went slowly out of him, as he watched the average of deceleration develop steadily hour by dragging hour. It grew increasingly clear that, above three hundred and fifty million miles a second, increases and decreases in speed must be governed by far more potent laws than they were here. Four times as much at least, though there seemed to be an upper limit.

As the days dragged by, Hedrock watched the light on the speedometer grow darker, darker, until the beam of force quivered gently, and stopped.

He was lost. Lost in a night that grew more meaningless every hour. He slept restlessly, then returned to the control chair.

He had barely settled into it when there was a jar that shook every plate in the lifeboat. The little craft spun like driftwood in a whirlpool. It was the chair that saved Hedrock, the all-purpose chair. Light as thistledown, it twisted as fast as the ship, holding him always downward and steady; and with him the entire control board.

The surrounding space was aswarm with monstrously large torpedo-shaped ships. Every 'stat showed dozens of the mile-long things; and each stupendous machine was drawn up as part of a long line that completely enveloped his small craft. Out of that mass of machines came a thought. It boiled into the control room like an atomic gas bubble. It was so strong that, for an instant, it had no coherency. And even when it did, it was a long moment before Hedrock's staggered mind grasped that the titanic thought was not for him, but *about* him.

"—an inhabitant of ... ! ! ! —meaningless ,, . Intelligence type nine hundred minus. ,.. Study value Tension 1,... Shall it be destroyed?"

The mad, private thought that came to Hedrock, as he sat there with tottering reason, was that this was the relation-value of all that desperate fighting on Earth to suppress the interstellar drive. It didn't matter. It was too late. Man was too slow by a measureless time. Greater beings had long since grasped all of the universe that they desired, and the rest would be doled out according to their savage will, ... Too late, too late—

11

IT COULD HAVE BEEN ONE MINUTE OR MANY THAT PASSED AS Hedrock sat there. When he finally began to observe again, he had the sensation of emerging from darkness. His will to live surged up into a bright pattern of purpose. His gaze narrowed on the 'stat plates. They were like windows through which he peered out at the mass of spaceships that surrounded him. The fear that came was not for himself, but for man. There were so many, too many. The implication of their presence was deadly.

But he was alive. The conscious, second thought of life galvanized him. His fingers flashed toward the controls. He glanced along the sighting guides, aimed at an opening between two of the massive vessels, plunged home the adjustor, waited an instant for the lifeboat to swing into line—and deliberately snapped the white accelerator far over.

His mind made a pause, for there was darkness, a gulf of physical, not mental darkness. Hedrock tore the drive out of gear. He recalled after a blank moment that there had been the faintest tug of movement. Now, there was nothing—no ships, no stars. Nothing at all. It wasn't that the 'stats were blank. They were on. But they registered blackness unqualified by light. After a moment, he touched a button on the instrument board. Almost immediately a word glowed up at him. It said simply: Metal.

Metal! Surrounded by metal. That meant he was inside one

of the mile-long alien ships. Just how it had been done was a mystery, but if the Weapon Makers on Earth had a vibratory transmission system, whereby material objects could be sent through walls and over distances, then the absorption of his lifeboat into the hold of a bigger machine was well within the realm of possibility.

He felt torn by a soaring comprehension of his situation. He was obviously a prisoner, and in due course would learn his fate. They were letting him live—which must mean that he had been found of some value. Hedrock climbed into a spacesuit. He felt tense but very determined.

Ready finally, he opened the air lock, and stood for a moment thinking bleakly of how far he was from the earth. And then he stepped down and out. There was no gravity, and so he floated down under the impetus of a push on the lock. His flashlight blazed an intense path downward, revealing a flat plain of metal, with walls sharply delineated in the near distance, walls with doors in them.

The picture was normal, even ordinary. He need only try all the doors, and if one opened, follow through. The first door opened effortlessly. After a moment, his nervous reflexes caught up with his staggered mind, and he felt an intense wonder. He was staring down at a city from a height of about two miles. The city glittered and shone from a blaze of hidden light, and it was set in a garden of trees and shrubs in bloom. Beyond was green countryside, bright with a profusion of brush and meadows and sparkling streams. The whole curved gently upward into a haze of distance on the three sides that he could see. Except for the limited horizon, it could have been Earth.

The second tremendous shock struck Hedrock at that point. A city, he thought, an Earth-like city in a ship so big that—his mind couldn't grasp it. The spaceship, which had seemed a mile long, was actually at least fifty, and it was cruising through space with several hundred of its kind, each machine the size of a planetoid, and manned by superbeings.

Hedrock remembered his purpose. He held his thought on a cold, practical level as he estimated the size of the largest door. It seemed to him that it was large enough. He went back to the lifeboat. He had a moment of doubt as to whether the mysterious beings would permit it to move. It all depended on what they wanted him to do. His doubt ended as the little machine slipped gently forward, cleared the door by serveral feet, and landed a few minutes later on the outskirts of the city.

Safely landed, he sat there, letting the unpleasant thrill tingle along his nerves, the realization that this was what they wanted. There was no doubt that some over-all purpose was

77

being worked on him; and while precautions seemed ridiculous, nevertheless they must be taken. He tested the atmosphere. Air pressure was slightly over fourteen pounds, oxygen content was nineteen percent, nitrogen seventy-nine percent, temperature seventy-four, and gravitational pressure 1G. He stopped there, because the figures were the same as for Earth.

Hedrock divested himself of his spacesuit. The possibility of resistance did not exist. Creatures who could casually, in minutes, recreate an Earth setting for him had him, *had* him. He stepped out of the lifeboat into silence. Ahead were empty streets that stretched on every side, a deserted city. There was not a breeze, not a movement. The nearby trees stood in the deathly quiet, their leaves curled stiffly, their branches steady. It was like a scene under glass, a garden in a bottle, and he the tiny figure standing rigidly. Only he wasn't going to stand there.

He came to a white, glistening building, wide and long but not very high. His knock made a hollow sound, and after a moment he tried the latch. The door opened and revealed, without any preliminary of vestibule or hallway, a small metal room. There was a control board, and a multipurpose chair, and a man sitting in the chair. Hedrock stopped as he saw that it was he, himself, sitting there, and that this was a replica of his spaceboat. Hedrock walked forward stiffly, half expecting the body to vanish as he approached. But it didn't. He expected his hand to pass through that false version of his own body. *But it didn't.* The feel of the clothes was unmistakable, and the flesh of the face was warm with life as he touched it with his fingers. The Hedrock who was in the chair paid no attention but continued to stare fixedly at the general 'stat plate.

Hedrock followed that intent gaze, and sighed when he saw the Empress' passionately earnest face image on it. So they were re-enacting Innelda's final order to him, without sound effects, without her vibrant voice urging him to land the spaceboat. He waited, wondering what was next on the program, but though several minutes went by the scene did not change.

His patience was considerable, but finally he backed away toward the door. Outside, he paused to realize how rigid his muscles had become. It was a figment that he had seen, he told himself tautly, a scene out of his memory recreated in some fashion. But why that scene? Why any?

On impulse he opened the door again, and peered inside. The room was empty. He closed the door, walked swiftly into the city, and felt the silence again like a pall around him. Slowly, he relaxed. Because he must face every facet of strangeness that his unseen captors had in store for him.

78

Something about him had roused their interest, and it was up to him to force issues and so hold their attention until he had discovered the secret of their control over him.

Hedrock turned abruptly into the imposing entrance of a thirty-story marble skyscraper. The ornate door opened like the one in the first building he had entered, not into an ante-room, but directly into a room. It was a larger chamber than the first. There were guns in floor and wall showcases, and in the corner sat a man opening a letter. The first shock had already come to Hedrock. This was the Linwood Weapon Shop, and the man in the corner was Daniel Neelan. The interview scene between Neelan and himself was about to be re-enacted.

He walked forward, conscious that something was wrong with the picture. It was not quite as he remembered it. He realized abruptly what was wrong. Neelan had not been reading a letter when they first met.

Was it possible that this was something that had happened afterwards?

As he paused directly behind the seated Neelan, and glanced at the letter the other was holding, Hedrock realized that it was very possible indeed. The envelope had a Martian post-office mark on it. This was the mail that the Weapon Shops had offered to obtain for Neelan, and this was Neelan *after* the two of them had been to 1874 Trellis Minor Building.

But how was it being done? It was one thing to build up a scene which they had obtained from his memory, quite another to enact something in which he had not participated, and which had taken place countless light years away, and nearly two months ago. Yet there must be a reason why they were performing so difficult a feat for his benefit. He decided that his captors wanted him to read the letter that Neelan had received.

He was bending forward to read it when there was a momentary blur before his eyes. It ended, and he realized he was sitting down instead of standing, and that he himself was now holding the letter. The changeover was so startling that Hedrock involuntarily turned in the chair and looked behind him.

For long moments he stared at the body of himself that stood there, rigid, leaning slightly forward, eyes fixed and un-winking; and then, slowly, he faced about again, and stared down—at Neelan's clothes, Neelan's hands and Neelan's body. He began to feel the difference, to become aware of Neelan's thoughts and intense emotional interest in the letter.

Before Hedrock could more than realize that somehow—somehow—*his* "mind" had been put into Neelan's body, Nee-

Ian was concentrating on the letter. It was from his brother Gil, and it read:

Dear Dan:

Now I can tell you about the greatest invention in the history of the human race.

I had to wait till now, a few hours before we leave, because we could not take the risk of the letter being intercepted. We want to present the world with a *fait accompli*. When we come back, we intend to shout our news from the housetops, and have endless film and other records to support our story. But to get down to facts.

There are seven of us, headed by the famous scientist, Derd Kershaw. Six of us are science specialists. The seventh is a fellow called Greer, a sort of general handy man who keeps the books and the records, who turns on the automatic cookers, and so on. Kershaw is teaching him how to operate the controls, so that the rest of us can be relieved of that chore—

Hedrock-Neelan paused there, sick to his soul. "The children!" he muttered huskily. "Those damned grown-up children." After a moment he thought: *So Greer was a handy man. No wonder the man had known nothing about science.*

He was about to read on, when Hedrock momentarily disentangled his ego from that compound awareness. He thought, almost blankly, *But Neelan didn't know about Greer. How could he have a feeling about him?* That was as far as he got. Neelan's compulsion to continue reading the letter overwhelmed his will to separate thought. *They* read on:

I got into the affair as a result of Kershaw noticing an article of mine in the Atomic Journal, in which I described that I had been doing some contraterrene research exactly along the lines of an idea that he had for the development of his invention.

Right here I might as well say that the chance of this discovery being duplicated by other researchers is practically nil. It embraces, in its conception, too many specialized fields. You know what we were taught during our training period, that there are nearly five hundred thousand special science fields, and that undoubtedly by skilful coordination of knowledges countless new inventions would be forthcoming, but that no known mind training could ever coordinate a fraction of these sciences, let alone all of them.

I mention this to emphasize once again the importance of secrecy. Kershaw and I had a midnight conference, and I was hired under the most confidential terms.

Dan, listen—the news is absolutely stupendous. We've got a drive that's so fast it's like a dream. The stars are conquered. Almost as soon as I finish this letter, we leave for Centaurus.

I feel sick and shaky and cold and hot at the mere idea of it. It means everything. It's going to blow the world wide open. Just think of all those people who were forcibly dumped on Mars and Venus and the various moons—it had to be done, of course; somebody had to live there and exploit their wealth—but now there's hope, a new chance on greener, finer worlds.

From this point onward, man will expand without limit, and put an end forever to all those petty murderous squabbles over ownership of property. Henceforth, there will always be more than enough.

The reason we have to be so careful is that the Isher Empire will be shaken to its foundations by the unprecedented emigration that would begin immediately, and the Empress Innelda will be the first to realize, the first to attempt our destruction. We're not even sure that the Weapon Shops will support such a change. After all, they are an integral part of the Isher set-up; they have provided the checks and balances, and so have helped to create the most stable governmental system ever devised for unstable man. For the time being we prefer that they also do not find out what we have.

One more thing: Kershaw and I have discussed the possible effect of light years of distance on your and my sensory relation. He thinks that our speed of withdrawal from the solar system will give the effect of an abrupt break, and of course there will be the agony of acceleration. We—

Neelan stopped there. Because that was what he had felt, the agony, then the break! Gil *wasn't dead*. Or rather—his mind rushed on—Gil hadn't died that day a year ago. Somewhere during the journey Greer had—

At that point, Hedrock once more tore his own consciousness clear of that integrated reaction. "My God," he thought shakily, "we're a part of each other. He's having emotions based on my knowledge, and I'm experiencing the emotions as if they're my own. It would be understandable if I was his brother, with whom he had long had an established sensory relationship. But I'm not. I'm a stranger, and we've only met once."

His thought paused there. Because it was possible that to the alien scientists who were manipulating their two minds and bodies, there was no more difference between Neelan and himself than there had been between the Neelan twins. After all, most human nervous systems were structurally similar. If the two Neelans could be "attuned" to each other, then apparently so could any two human beings.

This time, having rationalized it, Hedrock offered no resistance to the re-merging of their separate identities. He expected to finish reading Gil's letter. But instead the letter blurred. Hedrock-Neelan blinked, and then he started violently as fine, hot sand laced against his face.

He saw that he was no longer in the weapon shop, and there was no sign of the phantom city. He twisted in a spasm of muscular reaction and realized that he was lying on a flat red desert under an enormous bulging sun. Far to his left, through a thick haze of dust, was another sun. It seemed to be farther away and was smaller, but it looked almost the color of blood in that world of powdered sand. Men lay nearby on the sand. One of them turned weakly; he was a big, fine looking fellow, and his lips moved. There was no sound, but in a curious fashion his turning the way he did brought into Neelan-Hedrock's line of vision boxes, crates and metal structures. Hedrock recognized a water-making machine, a food case and a telestat. His observation was interrupted.

"Gil!" he shrieked. Or rather, it was Neelan's reaction. "Gil, *Gil*, GIL!"

"Dan!" It seemed to come from far away. It was more a wisp of thought in his mind than a sound. It was a tired sigh that bridged the great night. It began again, faint, far-away but clear, and directed at Neelan, "Dan, you poor mug, where are you? Dan, how are you doing this? I don't feel that you're close. . . . Dan, I'm a sick man, dying. We're on a freak planet that's going to pass close to one of the Centauri suns. The storms will grow worse, the air hotter. We—oh, God!"

The break was so sharp, it hurt like fire. It was like an over-stretched elastic—giving. Countless light years rushed in to fill the gap. Hedrock realized that "they" had not actually been at the scene. It had been a sensory connection between the two brothers, and the picture of that nightmarish world had come through the eyes of Gil Neelan.

Whoever was doing this had achieved a fantastic control and understanding of human beings. It took a long moment to realize that Neelan was still in the Weapon Shop, and still clutching the letter. There were tears in his eyes, but presently it was possible to see the letter again, and to finish reading it:

. . . We will probably be completely separated for the first time since we were born. It's going to feel very empty and lonely.

I know you're envying me, Dan, as you read this. When

I think how long man has dreamed of going to the stars, and how it had been proved time and again that it can't be done, I know exactly how you feel. Particularly you who were the adventurer of our family.

Wish me luck, Dan, and watch your tongue.

Your other half,

Gil.

Just when the transformation occurred, or by what stages, Hedrock wasn't sure. His first awareness of change was that he was no longer in the Weapon Shop. That was not immediately important to him. His mind was caught up in thought of Gil Neelan and of the miracle that had been wrought. Somehow, these mighty captors of his had intensified the flimsy bonds between the two brothers, and made a thought connection across light-centuries, an incredible, instantaneous connection.

And, casually, *he* had been taken along on that fantastic journey.

Odd, how dark it was. Since he was not in the Weapon Shop, he should logically be back in the "city", or somewhere on the ship of the beings who had captured him. Hedrock lifted himself, and by that action realized that he had been lying face downward. As he moved, his hands and feet tangled in a network of intertwined ropes. He had to grab at the individual strands of rope to balance himself. He swayed there in pitch darkness.

He had been holding himself calm, fighting with all his strength to comprehend each separate experience. But this one was too much. Panic struck him like a physical blow. Instead of a floor there was a mesh of ropes like the rigging in the ships that sailed the seas of Earth in olden days, or like the web of some nightmare-sized spider. His thought paused, and a chill spread down his spine. *Like a spider's web.*

A vague blueish light began to grow around him, and he saw that the city was indeed gone. In its place was an unearthly dark-blue world, and webs, miles and miles of webs. They reared up toward the remote ceiling and vanished into the distance of the dimness. They spread out in all directions, fading into the semi-night like things of some nether world. And, mercifully, they did not appear to be inhabited at first.

Hedrock had time to brace his brain for the most terrible shock its highly trained structure would ever have to face. He had time to grasp that this was the interior of the ship, and that there *must* be inhabitants. Far above him, there was suddenly a flicker of movement. Spiders. He saw them plainly, huge things with many legs, and grew tense with the bitterness of his realization. So a tribe of spider-like beings were Nature's prize package, the supreme intelligence of the ages, rulers of the universe. The thought seemed to be in his mind a very long time, before a faint light focussed on him from a hidden source. Abruptly, a very thunderbolt of mind vibrations rocked his brain:

"—examination negative.... There is no physical connection between these beings ... energy only—"

"But the tensions were augmentable by energy. The connection was contrived across—xxx?!! distance."

"—my finding is that there is no physical connection—" Coldly.

"I was merely expressing amazement, mighty xx—!! (meaningless name). Here is undoubtedly a phenomenon closely related to the behavior of this race. Let us ask him—"

"MAN!"

Hedrock's brain, already strained under the weight of those enormous thoughts, cringed before that direct wave. "Yes?" he managed finally. He spoke aloud. His voice made a feeble sound against the blue-dark vastness, and was swallowed instantly by the silence.

"MAN, WHY DID ONE BROTHER MAKE A LONG JOURNEY TO FIND OUT WHAT HAD HAPPENED TO THE OTHER BROTHER?"

For a moment the question puzzled Hedrock. It seemed to refer to the fact that Dan Neelan had come from a remote meteor to the earth to find out why the sensory connection with his brother Gil had been broken. It seemed a fairly meaningless question, because the answer was so obvious. They were brothers, they had been brought up together, they had a very special intimate relationship. Before Hedrock could explain the simple elements of human nature involved, the titanic thunder raged down again at his mind:

"MAN, WHY DID YOU RISK YOUR LIFE SO THAT OTHER HUMAN BEINGS CAN GO TO THE STARS? AND WHY DO YOU WANT TO GIVE THE SECRET OF IMMORTALITY TO OTHERS?"

In spite of the tattered state of Hedrock's thoughts understanding began to streak through. These spider beings were trying to comprehend man's emotional nature *without having themselves a capacity for emotion*. Here were blind things asking to have color explained to them, stone-deaf creatures being given a definition of sound. The principle was the same.

What they had done was explained now. The apparently meaningless re-enactment of the scene between himself and the Empress had been designed so that his emotions could be

84

observed while he was risking his life for an altruistic purpose. In the same way and for a similar reason, the sensory connection had been established between the Neelans and himself. They wanted to measure and assess emotions in action.

Once more a clamor of outside thought interrupted him: "IT IS REGRETTABLE THAT ONE OF THE BROTHERS DIED, BREAKING THE CONNECTION—"

"THAT NEED BE NO DETERRENT. NOR IS THE BROTHER ON EARTH NEEDED, NOW THAT WE HAVE ESTABLISHED A DIRECT CONNECTION BETWEEN OUR PRISONER AND THE DEAD ONE. A MAJOR EXPERIMENT IS IN ORDER—"

"X-XX?!X PROCEED AT ONCE."

"WHAT IS TO BE DONE FIRST?"

"GIVE HIM FREEDOM, OF COURSE."

There was a prolonged pause, then a blur. Hedrock grew taut, and involuntarily closed his eyes. When he opened them again, he saw that he was in one of his secret laboratories on earth, the one in which the giant rat had nearly killed him.

12

HE *seemed* TO BE BACK ON THE EARTH. HEDROCK CLIMBED gingerly to his feet, and examined himself. He was still wearing the insulation suit, which Greer had given him, and in which he had dressed himself before leaving the lifeboat to wander around in the earth-like "city" the spider beings had created for him. He looked around the room slowly, searching for tiny discrepancies that would indicate that this was another illusion.

He couldn't be sure. And yet he felt different than when they had been manipulating him. Then there had been an over-all atmosphere of unreality. He had been like a man in a dream. He no longer felt that way.

He stood frowning, remembering the last thoughts he had received from them. One of the beings had definitely indicated that he was to be given his freedom for the next phase of their experiment. Hedrock was not sure what they meant by freedom, because it was clear that they were still studying human emotional behavior. But he had been in danger so often in his life that, in the final issue, he did not allow personal fear to alter his purpose. He did however want to test the reality of his surroundings.

He walked to the general 'stat in one of the study rooms, and tuned into a news channel. It was a drab account to which he listened then. The commentator was concerned with some new laws which were under discussion by the Imperial Parliament. There was no mention of the interstellar drive. If there had been any excitement at the time of his escape from Kershaw's ship it had apparently died down. Whatever effort had been made to force the Empress to give up the secret seemed to have been abandoned.

He shut off the 'stat, and changed into a "business" suit. Carefully, he selected four more ring weapons, and then, arrayed for battle, he stepped through a transmitter into one of his apartments in Imperial City. He began to feel a lot better. In the back of his mind he had plans for experiments *he* was going to conduct if the spider beings tried to take control of him again, but he was still anxious about the exact nature of the "freedom" he had been given. He hurried to the great window that overlooked the city looking south. For more than a minute Hedrock gazed at the familiar scene of the tremendous metropolis; and then, turning slowly, he walked over to the apartment 'stat, and called Public News Service.

The news organization was associated with the Weapon Shops, and provided free information and news. The girl who talked to Hedrock answered all his questions without asking his identity. From her he learned definitely that the Empress had publicly and repeatedly denied all knowledge of an interstellar drive, and that the Weapon Shops after two weeks of intense propaganda against her had dropped their campaign abruptly.

Hedrock broke the connection grimly. So Innelda had gotten away with it. He could understand why the Weapon Shops had ceased putting pressure on her. Theirs would be an increasingly unpopular cause, for they had no evidence to offer; and they were too logical to pursue openly a matter which might turn people against them. It could be taken for granted that ninety per cent of the population would long ago have lost interest in the affair. Of those who remained, the majority wouldn't know what to do, even if they believed that the drive existed. How did one force the hereditary ruler of the solar system to give up a secret?

Hedrock, who had his own ideas of how it would have to be done, became grimmer. He moved across to the library, and studied the century clock. He had several problems. It would take a little while to organize his campaign, and his time of action must be postponed until a Rest Day.

As for the spider beings, they were an unknown factor,

whose movements he could not control. He'd have to act as if they did not exist.

"Let's see now," he muttered half to himself, "today is October 1st, and tomorrow is—*Rest Day!*"

That shocked him. It meant that he had one afternoon to prepare for the most sustained physical effort in his career. What disturbed him was that the preliminary would not be at all simple. Imagine facing men like Nensen, Deely and Triner when he was in a hurry. But there was no time to waste in regret that the situation wasn't different.

He returned to his underground laboratory, and began a detailed study of a very large 'stat which occupied one corner of his transport room. The 'stat was lined with row on row of glow points, slightly more than fifteen hundred. It took a while to punch out the score of individual numbers that he wanted. Seventeen of them turned a rich green. The other three flashed red, which meant that the three men at the other end were not in their offices. Seventeen out of twenty was better than he had expected. Hedrock straightened from his job of selection, and faced the 'stat as it started to glow.

"Take a good look at me," he said, "You will probably be seeing me today."

He paused, considering his next words. It would be foolish to indicate that he was talking to more than one individual. Undoubtedly, some of the shrewd men listening in probably knew that other firms were in the same position as their own, but it would be gratuitous folly to confirm their suspicion.

Satisfied, Hedrock went on, "Your firm will remain open until tomorrow morning. Provide sleeping quarters, entertainment and food for the staffs. Continue with normal business until the usual hour, or until further notice. Employees must be paid a twenty percent bonus for this week. For your private information, a great emergency has arisen, but if you do not hear further by seven A.M. tomorrow, consider the matter closed. Meanwhile, read Article 7 of your incorporation papers. That is all."

He clicked off the 'stat and grimaced at the lateness of the hour. At least thirty minutes must lapse between his verbal and his first physical call. There was no other way. It was impossible that he appear in person a minute after his 'stat message. The message would have caused a big enough sensation as it was, without the added complication of his immediate arrival.

Besides, he still had to rig up a magnifier control, and swallow the magnifier. He stood finally with narrowed eyes, considering the potentialities of the interviews that he had to make. Some of the executives out there would be extremely hard to dominate quickly. He had been intending to take action against several of them for a long time. They'd been big bosses too long. His policy of letting a family operate for generations, merely paying into a central fund, but otherwise without control, had progressively weakened his authority. It couldn't be helped. Control of so many was a practical impossibility.

The half-hour up, Hedrock plugged in a transmitter, examined the gleaming corridor that showed beyond. He stepped through. The door he finally came to had a sign on it:

STAR REALITY CO.
TRILLION CREDITS IN PROPERTIES
Office of the President
J. T. TRINER
Trespassers Forbidden

With his ring, Hedrock actuated the secret mechanism of the door. He walked in, straight past the pretty girl at the great reception desk, who tried to stop him. The rays of his ring automatically unlocked the second door. He stepped inside to find himself in a large and imposing office. A big pale-faced, pale-eyed man rose from behind a curving monster of a desk, and stared at him.

Hedrock paid no attention. One of the other rings that he had put on his finger was tingling violently. He turned his hand slowly. When the tingling stopped, the ring stone was pointing directly at the wall behind the desk. It was a good job of camouflage, Hedrock decided admiringly. The wall design was unbroken, the enormous blaster behind it perfectly hidden. Without his finder ring, he would never have spotted it.

Abruptly, he felt grimmer. He allowed himself the icy and swift thought that his discovery only confirmed his opinion of the man. A veritable cannon hidden in his office—what damnable stuff! His private case history of Triner showed that he wasn't merely self-centered and ruthless, common traits in an age of gigantic administration trusts. Nor was he simply amoral; hundreds of thousands of Isher citizens had committed as many murders as Triner, but the difference in motive was like the difference between right and wrong. Triner was a prurient wretch, a lecherous skunk, a very hound of evil.

The man was coming forward, holding out his hand, a hearty smile on his pale face, a hearty tone to his voice, as he said, "I don't know whether to believe in you or not, but at least I'm willing to listen."

Hedrock strode toward the outstretched hand as if to shake

88

it. At the last instant, he stepped past the man and in a moment had seated himself in the big chair behind the curving desk. He faced the startled executive, thinking savagely: So Triner was willing to talk, was he? That was nice. But first he'd get some psychological bludgeoning and a lesson in straightforward ruthlessness with emphatic punctuation of the fact that there were tougher men in the world than J. T. Triner. Keep pushing him; keep him off balance. Hedrock said curtly:

"Before you sit down *in that chair*, Mr. Triner, before we talk, I want you to start your staff on the job you're going to do for me—are you listening?"

There was no doubt about it. Triner was not only listening, he was shocked and angry and bewildered. Not that he looked cowed. Hedrock knew better than to expect fear. Triner's expression simply grew cautious, with a mixture of curiosity thrown in. He said, "What is it you want done?"

That was too important for ruthlessness of manner. Hedrock drew a folded paper from his pocket. "There," he said earnestly, "are the names of fifty cities. I want all my business properties in those cities listed according to avenues and streets. Never mind who's in them. Just get the street numbers, two, four, six, eight and so on. And only in cases where there are many in a row, such as a whole block, at least a dozen altogether. Do you follow that?"

"Yes, but—" Triner looked dazed. Hedrock cut him off:

"Give the order." He studied the man from narrowed eyes, then he leaned forward. "I—hope—Triner—that you have been living up to Article 7 of your constitution."

"But, man, that article was promulgated nearly a thousand years ago. You can't mean—"

"Can you provide that list, or can't you?"

Triner was sweating visibly. "I guess so," he said finally. "I really don't know. I'll see." He stiffened abruptly, added through clenched teeth, "Damn you, you can't come in here and—"

Hedrock realized when he had pushed a man far enough. "Give the order," he said mildly, "then we'll talk."

Triner hesitated. He was a badly shaken man, and, after a moment, he must have realized that he could always countermand any instructions. He said, "I'll have to use the desk 'stat."

Hedrock nodded and watched and listened while the order was transmitted to an underling chief. He then smirked at Hedrock.

"What's the dope?" he asked in a confidential tone. "What's it all about?"

The man's seeming acquiescence gave him away. Hedrock sat icily thoughtful. So the controls of the gun were *in* the desk,

89

somewhere beside where Triner had drawn his chair. Hedrock studied the physical situation thoughtfully. He was sitting at the desk, his back to the cannon, and with Triner to his left. The door leading to the outer office was about fifty feet away, and beyond it was the reception girl. The wall and door would protect her. Anybody else who came in would have to be kept well to the left, preferably behind and beside Triner. Hedrock nodded with satisfaction. His gaze had never left Triner; and now he said:

"I'm going to tell you everything, Triner—" that was an appetizer for the man's undoubted curiosity, and should restrain his impatience. Hedrock went on—"but first I want you to do one more thing. You have an executive accountant in the head office here, named Royan. Ask him to come up. After I've spoken to him, you'll have a better idea as to whether he'll be in the firm after today."

Triner looked puzzled, hesitated, and then spoke briefly into the 'stat. A very clear, resonant voice promised to come up immediately. Triner clicked off, and leaned back in his chair. "So you're the man behind that mysterious wall 'stat," he temporized finally.

He waved his hand at the design on the wall beside him, then said suddenly, his voice intense, "Is the Empress behind us? Is it the House of Isher that owns this business?"

"No!" said Hedrock.

Triner looked disappointed, but said, "I'm going to believe that, and do you know why? The House of Isher needs money too badly and too continuously to let a treasure like this company vegetate the way it's been doing. All that stuff about dividing the profits with the tenants periodically, whatever else it is, it isn't Isher."

"No, it isn't Isher," said Hedrock. And watched the baffled look that came into Triner's face. Like so many men before him, Triner didn't quite dare defy the secret owner so long as there was a possibility that the owner was the Imperial family. And Hedrock had found that denial only increased the doubts of the ambitious.

There was a knock at the door, and a young man of about thirty-five came in. He was a big chap with a brisk manner. his eyes widened a little as he took in the seating arrangement of the men in the private office. Hedrock said:

"You're Royan?"

"Yes." The young man glanced at Triner questioningly, but Triner did not look up.

Hedrock motioned to the decoration that was the wall telestat. "You have been previously informed as to the meaning behind this 'stat?"

90

"I've read the incorporation articles," Royan began; and then he stopped. Understanding poured into his eyes. "You're not that—"

"Let us," said Hedrock, "have no histrionics. I want to ask you a question, Royan?"

"Yes?"

"How much money—" Hedrock articulated his words "did Triner take out of the firm last year?"

There was a little hiss of indrawn breath from Triner, then silence. Finally, Royan laughed softly, an almost boyish laugh, and said, "Five billion credits, sir."

"That's a little high, isn't it," Hedrock asked steadily, "for a salary?"

Royan nodded. "I don't think Mr. Triner regarded himself as being on salary, but rather as an owner."

Hedrock saw that Triner was staring fixedly down at the desk, and his right hand was moving casually toward a tiny ornamental statue.

Hedrock said, "Come over here, Royan." He motioned with his left hand, waited until the young man had taken up a position to the left of Triner, and then manipulated the ring control of his own magnifier. The magnification involved was small, not more than an inch all around. He could have gained the same physical effect by sitting up and swelling out his chest. What was important about it was that it changed the basic structure of his "business" suit and of his own body. Both became virtually as impregnable as a weapon shop itself.

Almost everything that had happened to him after his escape from the Weapon Makers was the result of his not being able to wear the suit into a weapon shop.

Hedrock felt the greater rigidity of his body and his throat was stiffer, his voice slower, as he said, "I would say the salary was much too high. See that it is cut down to five million."

There was a wordless sound from Triner, but Hedrock went on speaking to Royan in that slow, steely voice, "Furthermore, in spite of its co-operative structure, this firm has acquired an unenviable reputation for remorselessness, and the policy of its president of having pretty women picked up in the street and taken to his various secret apartments is—"

He saw the final movement as Triner convulsively grasped the statuette. Hedrock stood up, as Royan yelled a warning.

The fire from the cannon disintegrated the chair on which Hedrock had sat, spumed off the metal desk, drenched the ceiling with flame. It was immensely violent, at least ninety thousand cycles of energy, but it was not so strong that Hedrock did not notice the flash of Royan's gun. After a moment, the sequence of events was clear. Triner had manipulated and fired the cannon at Hedrock, then whirled, drawing his imperial gun with the intention of killing Royan. But Royan, using a Weapon Shop defensive model, had fired first.

Where Triner had been was a shiningness that twinkled and faded instantly as the powerful suction pumps (automatically set off by the cannon) drew great gulps of fresh air through the room. It was a standard process, so swift that the total volume of air in the room was actually changed five times a second.

In the office, between Hedrock and Royan, silence settled. "I don't see," said Royan finally, "how you escaped."

Hedrock swiched off his magnification, said hurriedly:

"You're the new president of the company, Royan. Your salary is five million a year. What kind of mind-training course are you giving your son?"

Royan was recovering more rapidly than Hedrock had expected. "The usual," he said.

"Change it. The Weapon Shops have recently published the details of a new course, which is not very popular as yet. It includes the strengthening of moral functions. But now ... when will the lists be ready that Triner ordered for me? Or don't you know about them?"

The speed of the conversation seemed to be dazing Royan again, but he carried the load. "Not before six. I—"

Hedrock cut him off. "You are going to get some awful shocks tomorrow, Royan, but bear up. Don't lose your head. We have incurred the wrath of a powerful secret organization. We are to be given a lesson. There will be great destruction of our property, but do not under any circumstances let on to anyone that it *is* our property, nor begin reconstruction for a month, or until further notice."

He finished grimly, "We must take our losses without outcry. Fortunately, tomorrow is Rest Day. The people will be away from their shops. But remember, have—those—lists—ready—at—six!"

He left the man abruptly. The reference to a secret organization was as good a story as any, and when the giant started moving, all its weaknesses would be dwarfed by the horrendous reality. But first, now, some other calls, a few of the easier ones, then eat, then the arrogant Nensen, and then take action on the vastest scale.

He killed Nensen an hour later by the simple method of reflecting the energy of the man's own gun back at him. The once indomitable Deely turned out harmless, a reformed monster of an old man who resigned swiftly when he saw that Hedrock was not interested in so delayed a conversion. The other men were obstacles whose curiosity and mental inertia had to be overcome. It was a quarter to seven the next morning when Hedrock took an energy drug, several vitamin shots and lay down for half an hour to let them work on his weary body.

He ate an enormous breakfast, and a few minutes before eight o'clock adjusted the magnifier of his "business" suit to full power. The day of the giant had come.

13

A FEW MINUTES BEFORE THE FIRST NEWS CAME THROUGH Innelda was saying coldly, "Why do we always need money? Where does it go? Our annual budget is astronomical, and yet all I ever see are statements showing that so much of it goes for one general department and so much of it for another, and so on *ad nauseum*. The solar system is wealthy beyond estimate; the daily turnover at the Exchange runs into hundreds of billions of credits; and yet the government has no money. What's the matter? Are tax receipts in arrears?"

There was silence. The lord of finance glanced helplessly around the long cabinet table. His gaze came to rest finally on the face of Prince del Curtin. His eyes lighted up with silent appeal. The Prince hesitated, and then said:

"These cabinet meetings are beginning to follow a pattern, your Majesty. The rest of us are silent while you nag us. These days you have the perpetual complaining tone of a wife who, having spent all her husband's money, berates him for not having more."

She was slow in realizing the implications of that. She was so accustomed to plain speaking in private from her cousin that it did not strike her immediately that this comment was being made during an official meeting of the cabinet. She noted absently that the other men seemed relieved, but she was concentrating too hard on her own words for the full meaning to penetrate. She went on angrily:

"I am tired of being told that we haven't the money to carry on the normal expenses of government. The Imperial household expenses have been the same for generations. Any private property I have is maintained out of its earnings, and not by the State. I have been told many times that we have been taxing business and individuals to the limit, and that in fact business complains bitterly of the burden. If these astute business men would examine their books they would discover that there is another less obvious drain upon their resources. I refer to the levies of that outrageous, illegal organization, the Weapon Shops, which taxes the resources of this country fully as heavily as the legitimate government. Their pretense that they sell only guns is one of the greatest frauds ever perpetrated on a people. Their method is cunningly designed to enlist the support of grasping individuals among the unthinking masses. It is common knowledge that you need merely make an accusation that a business firm has swindled you, and the secret Weapon Shop courts will adjudicate for you. The question is, when does legitimate profit become a swindle? It is a purely philosophical problem, and could be argued endlessly. But these Shop courts all too easily assess triple damages, give half the money to the accuser, and keep the other half themselves. I tell you, gentlemen, we must start a campaign. We must convince business men that the Weapon Shops are a greater drain on them than is the government. Actually, of course, if business men were honest, it would make no difference. In such an event, the sanctimonious Weapon Makers would be exposed for the thieves they really are. Because, of course, they would still have to have money to maintain their organizations."

She paused, momentarily breathless, and remembered what Prince del Curtin had said earlier. She frowned at him. "So I sound like a nagging wife, do I, cousin? Having spent all my loving husband's money, I—"

She stopped short. She had a sudden, startled remembrance of the expression of relief that had come to the faces of the cabinet members after the Prince's comment. In a flash she realized what had not struck her before, that she had been personally accused in front of her whole cabinet.

"Well, I'll be damned!" she said explosively. "So I'm responsible. So I've been spending government money like an irresponsible woman—"

Once more she paused for breath. She was about to speak again when the 'stat beside her chair came to life. "Your Majesty, an urgent news message has just come through from the Middle West. A giant human being, one hundred and fifty feet tall, is destroying the business section of the city of Denar."

"What?"

"If you wish, I will show you the scene. The giant is retreating slowly before the attacks of mobile units."

"Never mind—" Her voice was cool and incisive. She finished her curt dismissal, "It must be some robotic machine built by a mad man, and the navy can handle it. I cannot give

94

the matter my attention at the moment. Report later."

"Very well."

During the silence that followed, she sat like a statue, her face whitely immobile, her eyes feeling hot in their sockets. She whispered finally, "Can it be some new action of the Weapon Shops?"

She hesitated, and then broke the thrall of what had happened. With a rush her mind came back to what she had been saying before the interruption. Her first words struck at the heart of the implied accusation.

"Prince, am I to understand that you hold me responsible in this public fashion for the financial predicament in which the government finds itself?"

The Prince was cool. "Your Majesty is misreading my words. My point was that these cabinet meetings have become nothing but scolding parties. The various departmental lords have a responsibility to parliament, and no useful purpose is served by destructive criticism."

She stared at him, and realized angrily that he had no intention of elaborating on his original statement. She said quickly, "Then you do not regard my suggestion that we inform business men of Weapon Shop thieving tactics—you do not regard that as constructive?"

The Prince was silent so long that she snapped, "Well, do you, or don't you?"

He stroked his jaw, and then looked directly at her. "No!" he said.

She stared at him wide-eyed, and breathless again. For this was being said in front of the entire cabinet. "Why not?" she said finally, in her most reasonable voice. "It would at least ease the pressure of criticism against us because taxes are so high."

"If it will make you happy," said Prince del Curtin, "it would probably do no harm to launch such a propaganda campaign. It shouldn't put us very much further in the red."

Innelda was cold again. "It has nothing to do with my happiness," she snapped. "I am thinking only of the State."

Prince del Curtin held his silence; and she gazed at him with a gathering determination. "Prince," she said earnestly, "you and I are related by blood. We are good friends in private, and we have had violent disagreements on many matters. However, now you have implied that I allow my private interests to intrude upon my responsibility to the State. Of course, I have always taken for granted that one cannot have two personalities, and that an individual's every act reflects to some extent his or her private prejudice. But there is a difference between unconscious assumptions which influence the individual's opinions—between that and a policy calculated to further the person's private ends. In what way have I become calculating? What made you suddenly utter a statement with so many implications? Well, I'm waiting."

"Suddenly is hardly the correct description," the Prince said drily. "For more than a month I have sat here listening with a gathering amazement to your impatient tirades. And I have asked myself one question. Would you like to know what that question is?"

The woman hesitated. The answer had already taken a turn that made her uneasy. She took the plunge. "Tell me."

"The question I asked myself," said Prince del Curtin, "was, 'What is bothering her? What decision is she trying to come to?' Now, the answer to that was not immediately obvious. We are all aware of your obsession with the Weapon Shops. On two different occasions you have been prepared to spend enormous sums of government money to further some action against the Weapon Shops. The first such incident occurred some years ago, and cost so much money that only last year was it paid off. And then a few months ago you began to make mysterious remarks to me, and you finally asked the cabinet to vote a large sum of money for a purpose which you did not then state, nor have you stated it since. Abruptly the fleet was called out, there was a charge made by the Weapon Makers that you had secured and were suppressing an interstellar drive. We financed a counter-propaganda, and eventually the affair fizzled out, although the cost as our budget figures show was colossal. I'd still like to know why you felt it necessary to have eight one-hundred-million cycle energy guns constructed at a cost of one billion eight hundred million credits each. Please don't misunderstand me. I am not asking you to explain that. I assume from certain remarks of yours that the incident was successfully concluded. The questions then remained: Why were you not satisfied? What was wrong? I decided that the problem was internal not external, personal not political."

The empty feeling was expanding inside her. But still she didn't know where he was heading. She hesitated, and was lost. The Prince continued:

"Innelda, you are thirty-two years old, and unmarried. There are rumors—forgive me for mentioning them—that you have lovers by the hundred, but I know for a fact that those rumors are false. Accordingly, to put it bluntly, it is damn well time you got married."

"Would you suggest," she asked in a voice that was just a little off key, "that I call forth all the young men of the land to perform deeds of derring-do, and that I marry the one who makes the best plum pudding?"

"That is quite unnecessary," said the Prince calmly. "You are already in love."

There was a stirring around the table. Smiles. Friendly faces. "Your Majesty," one man began, "this is the best news I've heard in—" He must have seen the expression on her face, because he faltered into silence.

She said, as if she had not heard the interruptions, "Prince, I am amazed. And who is the lucky young man?"

"Possibly one of the most formidable men whom I have ever met, but charming for all of his vitality and well worthy of your hand. He came to the palace about eight months ago, and you were immediately impressed with him, but unfortunately because of his antecedents, politically speaking, there was a conflict in your mind between your natural desires and your obsession."

She was aware now of whom he was talking, and she tried to head him off, "Surely, you are not referring to that young man whom I ordered hanged two months ago, but to whom I subsequently granted mercy."

Prince del Curtin smiled. "I admit your violent judgment against him puzzled me for a while, but actually it was merely another facet of the equally violent conflict going on in your mind."

Innelda was cool as she answered. "I seem to remember that you offered no great objections to the execution order."

"I was bowled over, I have an innate loyalty to your person, and your positive statements against him confused me. It was only afterwards that I realized it all fitted."

"You don't think I was sincere in giving the order?"

The Prince said, "In this world, people continually destroy those they love. They even commit suicide, thus destroying the one they love most of all."

"And what has all this to do with the conflict that is going on in my mind, and which—ironically—is making a shrew out of me?"

"Two months ago you told me that you had informed Captain Hedrock—" She tensed slightly as the name was mentioned for the first time—"that you would invite him back to the palace in two months. The time is up, and you cannot make up your mind to do so."

"You mean, my love has dimmed?"

"No." He was patient. "You have suddenly realized that calling him back would be an act far more significant than anything you imagined when you first named the time limit. In your mind it will be tantamount to an admission that the situation is exactly as I have stated."

Innelda stood up. "Gentlemen," she said with a faint, toler-
ant smile, "all this has been a revelation to me. I am sure that
my cousin means well, and in a way it might be an excellent
thing for me to get married. But I confess that I had never
thought of Captain Hedrock as the individual who would have
to hear my nagging all the rest of his life. Unfortunately,
there is another reason why I have hesitated to marry, and so
a third conflict should be added to the two mentioned by the
Prince. I—"

Beside her chair the telestat clicked on. "Your Majesty, the
Weapon Makers' Council has just issued a statement in connection with the giant."

Innelda sat down. She felt a vague shock at the realization
that she had forgotten about the meaningless titan with his
seemingly senseless program of destruction. Now she gripped
the edge of the long table. "I'll obtain a copy of it later," she
said. "What is the gist?"

There was a pause, and then another, deeper voice took
over: "A special statement has just been issued by the Weapon Makers' Council denouncing the hundred and fifty foot
giant, who has now devastated the business districts of the
cities of Denar and Lenton. The Weapon Makers state that the
rumor that the giant is a Weapon Shop machine is absolutely
false, and they emphasize that they will do all in their power
to help capture the giant. As was reported earlier, the giant
ran—"

She shut it off with a flick of her fingers. "Gentlemen," she
said, "I think you had all better go back to your headquarters
and stand by. The State is in danger, and this time—" She
stared at her cousin—"this time it does not seem to be a product of any calculation on my part."

She broke off. "Good day to you, gentlemen."

As was customary, the cabinet lords remained at their places
until she had left the room.

When she got back to her apartment, she waited a few minutes, and then put a call through to Prince del Curtin's office.
His face came onto the plate almost immediately. His eyes grew
questioning.

"Mad?" he asked.

"Of course not. You know better than that." She broke off.
"Del. is there any information yet as to what the giant wants?"

"He wants release of the interstellar drive."

"Oh! Then it is the Shops."

The Prince shook his head. "I don't think so, Innelda," he
said seriously. "They've issued a second statement within the
past few minutes, apparently realizing that their propaganda

of six weeks ago would be connected with the giant. They re-iterate their demand that you release the drive, but deny any connection with the giant, and once more offer to help catch him."

"Their denial is ridiculous on the face of it."

Prince del Curtin said earnestly, "Innelda, if this giant continues his destruction, you'll have to do something besides make accusations against the Shops."

"Are you coming down to breakfast?" she asked.

"No, I'm going to Denar."

She stared at him anxiously. "Be careful, Del."

"Oh, I have no intention of getting killed."

She laughed abruptly. "I'm sure of it. You can tell me later what your reason is for going."

"It's no secret. I've been invited by the navy. I think they want a responsible witness to the efforts they are making, so that no charges can later be made that they aren't doing everything in their power." He broke off. "So long."

"Goodbye," said Innelda. And clicked off her 'stat.

She felt tired, and so she lay down for an hour. And she must have slept, because she woke up to the sound of her private bedside 'stat. It was Prince del Curtin, looking and sounding very worried. "Innelda, have you been keeping track of the giant?"

She felt a sudden emptiness. It was still hard for her to grasp that such a menace had come out of nothingness only that morning, and was now threatening the nature of things Isher. She managed finally, "Is there anything special? I've been busy."

"Thirty-four cities, Innelda. Only one person killed yet, and that an accident. But think of it. It's real; it's no joke. The continent's beginning to boil like a toppled ant hill. He destroyed small establishments only, leaving the big companies untouched. A regular tidal wave of rumors have started about that, and I don't think any amount of propaganda is of value so long as that damned thing is at large." He broke off, "What is this about you hiding an interstellar drive? Is there any truth in it?"

She hesitated; then, "Why do you ask?"

"Because," he said grimly, "if it's true, and if that's what's behind the giant, then you'd better start thinking seriously of handing the secret over with the best possible grace. You can't stand another day of the giant."

"My dear—" she was cold, determined, "we'll stand a hundred days, if necessary. If an interstellar drive should be developed, the House of Isher would under present circumstances be opposed to it!"

99

"Why?"

"Because—" her voice was a resonant force, "our population would shoot off in all directions. In two hundred years, there'd be thousands of upstart royal families and sovereign governments ruling hundreds of planets, declaring wars like kings and dictators of old. And of all the people they would hate most would be the ancient House of Isher, whose living presence would make their loud pretensions ridiculous. Life on Earth would become one long series of wars against other star systems." She went on tautly, "It may seem silly to think of a situation as it would be two hundred years hence, but a family like ours, that has ruled in unbroken line for more than forty-seven hundred years, has learned to think in terms of centuries." She finished, "On the day that an administration method is developed whereby controlled stellar emigration is possible, on that day we could regard with approval such an invention. Until then—"

She stopped, because he was nodding, his lean, strong face thoughtful. "You're right, of course. That angle didn't occur to me. No chaos like that can be permitted. But our situation is becoming more serious every hour. Innelda, let me make a suggestion."

"Yes."

"You're going to be shocked."

A tiny frown creased her forehead. "Go ahead."

"All right. Listen: The Weapon Shops' propaganda is benefiting from the giant's handiwork, and at the same time they keep denouncing the giant. Let's take them up on that."

"What do you mean?"

"Let me get in touch with them. We've got to identify the people behind that giant."

"You mean, work with *them*?" She found her voice in an explosive outburst. "After three thousand years an Empress of Isher begs the aid of the Weapon Makers? Never!"

"Innelda, the giant is at the present moment destroying the city of Lakeside."

"Oh!"

She was silent. For the first time, she felt dismayed. Glorious Lakeside, second only to Imperial City in splendor and wealth. She tried to picture the shining giant crashing through the wonder city of lakes. And, slowly, she nodded agreement. There was no longer any doubt. After one short day, the giant, with a single exception, had become the most important factor in a shattering world.

She hesitated then, "Prince!"

"Yes."

"Captain Hedrock left me an address. Will you try to get in touch with him, and ask him to come to the palace, tonight if possible?"

Her cousin looked at her thoughtfully, said finally, simply, "What's the address?"

She gave it, and then sat back, forcing herself to relax. It was relieving after a minute to realize that she had made two great decisions.

It was a few minutes before five o'clock when the automatically relayed and recorded message from the Empress reached Hedrock. The request that he come to the palace startled him. It was hard to believe that Innelda had become so panicky about the future of the House of Isher.

He ended his destructive campaign, and returned to his secret laboratory. Arrived there, he tuned in to the secret wavelength of the Weapon Makers' Council, or rather the wavelength they thought secret; and, disguising his voice, said, "Members of the Weapon Makers' Council, I am sure that you have already realized the great advantage to your own cause of what the giants are doing."

It seemed to Hedrock that he must keep stressing that there were more than one involved. The Weapon Shops knew only too well that a normal human being was aged five years every thirty minutes when enlarged. He went on urgently, "The giants need immediate assistance. The Weapon Makers must now take over, must send out volunteers to play the role of giant for fifteen minutes, or half an hour per person. They do not have to destroy, but their appearance will give an effect of continuity. It is also important that the Shops now resume in full force their propaganda to compel the Empress to surrender the secret of the interstellar drive. It is essential that the first giant appear sometime early this evening. For the sake of the progressive forces of man, do not fail."

He was still in his hideout fifteen minutes later when the first of the giants appeared, so quick was the response. It was too quick. It showed private plans. It showed that the greatest power in the solar system was reacting like a finely poised steel spring; and he had no doubt that the plans included a determination to penetrate the identity of the person who knew their secrets. He was even prepared to believe that they knew who he was.

Accordingly, the time had come to bring into use one of his secret inventions. To begin with, he must make a trip through the one he had here in his hideout. Later, when the crisis came, he could make an attempt to utilize a replica that, long ago, he had secreted in the tombs of the palace. The next twelve hours would be decisive; and the great question was, would the spider beings let him carry through?

They showed no sign.

14

THE WARM, CLOUDY NIGHT WAS ABLAZE, THE LONG STREET, the notorious Avenue of Luck, scintillated like a jewel as Gonish walked along it. Mile on mile of jewels, fusing in the remote distance in either direction to a shimmer of mingled white and color. Signs glowed at the No-man, a glory of light-engraved messages:

WIN A FORTUNE
WALK IN WITH TEN CREDITS
WALK OUT WITH A MILLION

THE DIAMOND PALACE
10,000,000 DIAMONDS BLAZON
INTERIOR

TRY YOUR LUCK IN A
SETTING OF DIAMONDS

There were more of that type as Gonish walked on: THE RUBY PALACE—GOLD PALACE—EMERALD PALACE—intermingled with hundreds of no less gaudy structures. He came finally to his destination.

LUCKY EMPORIUM
BETS AS LOW AS FIVE PENNIES
NO LIMIT

The No-man paused, smiling gravely. It was fitting that the Empress had selected as their rendezvous one of her properties that catered to the masses. He must find out if she knew where Hedrock was, draw the information out of her, and escape with his life.

Gonish studied the crowds of predominantly young people who were streaming in and out of the garish building. Their laughter, the rich young voices of them, quickened the splendor of the blazing night. It all seemed normal, but he stood with practiced patience measuring the faces that moved by, assessing the characters of the loungers from their expressions; and it didn't take long to grasp the reality. The sidewalks

102

swarmed with Imperial Government agents.

Gonish stood grim. The Weapon Makers' Council had insisted that the place of meeting be public. It was understandable that the great precautions should be taken by the government secret police, and also that Her Majesty would not be anxious to have it known that she was dealing with the Weapon Shops so soon after the appearance of the giants. The conference was scheduled for the small hour of 2:30 A.M. It was now—Gonish glanced at his watch—exactly 1:55.

He remained where he was, conscious of a gathering sadness that it was his duty to attempt to ensnare Hedrock. But the identification of Hedrock from his message, as the man behind the giants had been shockingly convincing and, it seemed to Gonish, fully justifying the fears of the Council. Hedrock had shown by his actions that he was dangerous, and since he had made no attempt to explain his purposes when given the opportunity to do so, he must be considered guilty as charged.

It was unthinkable that a man who possessed the basic secrets of the Weapon Shops could be permitted at large. And if, as the Council believed, the Empress knew his whereabouts, the information would have to be cleverly extracted from her at the meeting which she herself had suggested. His friend Hedrock must die. And meanwhile he had better go inside and look around.

The interior sparkled with gardens and fountains and mechanical games. It was bigger than it had seemed from outside, both longer and wider. It was crowded with about equal numbers of men and women. Many of the women wore masks. Gonish nodded with comprehension. The Empress Isher would be simply one more masked woman. He paused before a game that was all flashing fire, a spray of violently glittering numbers twisting over the velvet blackness of a great board. Thoughtfully, the No-man watched several games run their course, trying each time to impress the over-all structure of the game into the ultra-trained region that was his brain. Finally, he placed ten credits on each of three numbers.

The fire slowed its gyrations in its coruscating fashion, and became a dazzling pillar of numbers piled one on top of another. The croupier intoned: "74, 29, 86, paying odds this time of 17 to 1."

As Gonish collected his five hundred ten credits, the croupier stared at him. "Say," he said in an astonished voice, "that's only the second time since I've been at this table that anybody's ever won on all three numbers."

The No-man smiled. "Mind over matter," he said gently; and, disinterested, wandered off. He could almost feel the croupier's astounded gaze boring into his back. What he wanted was a game he couldn't solve with his special abilities. And there was still nearly twenty-five minutes in which to find it. He came to an enormous machine with balls and an involved series of wheels under wheels. The balls, sixty of them, all numbered, started at the top, and, as the wheels spun, the balls rolled gradually downward, progressing from wheel to wheel. The farther down they went, the more they paid; but the first half of that complicated though swift journey didn't count, and few ever got lower.

The great attraction, so far as Gonish could make out, was the sensation of watching one's ball go down, down, with hope not fading until the last second. It turned out to be too simple. His ball went farthest four times in a row. Gonish pocketed his winnings, and came finally to a game that was a sphere of black and white light. The two lights merged into a single, spinning beam, and came out all white or all black. The bet was, which would it be?

Not once was he sure. He finally laid his first wager on the gambler's basis that white was the symbol of purity. White lost. He watched his money whisked off, and decided to forget the purity. Black lost. Beside him, a woman's rich laughter tinkled; and then, "I hope, Mr. Gonish, that you can do better than that with the giant. But please follow us to the private rooms."

Gonish turned. Three men and a woman stood there. One of the men was Prince del Curtin. The woman's face under its mask seemed long and the mouth itself was unmistakably Isher. Her eyes through the mask slits glinted green and her familiar, golden voice completed the recognition picture.

The No-man bowed low and said, "I'm sure I shall."

They went in silence to a luxuriously furnished drawing room, and sat down. Gonish took his time. There were questions he wanted to ask. The strange thing was, his casual references to Hedrock produced only silence. After a while, that was astounding. Gonish leaned back, studying the faces of the three men and the woman, genuinely disturbed. He said at last, very carefully, "My feeling is that you are withholding information."

It wasn't, he thought after he had spoken, that they could be doing it consciously. Their earnestness was unmistakable. And they couldn't possibly suspect that it was Hedrock he was after. Yet there seemed to exist among them a tacit understanding that nothing be said about Hedrock.

It was Prince del Curtin who made the denial. "I assure you, Mr. Gonish, you are quite mistaken. Among us four is every scrap of information that has come in about the giant. And, of course, any clue that may have turned up in the past as to his identity will probably be somewhere in our minds, too. You have only to ask the proper questions and we will answer."

It was convincing. This was going to be harder than he had thought, and it was just possible that, dangerous though it was, he might have to come out into the open. Gonish said slowly, "You are mistaken in assuming that you are the only reliable sources of information. There is a man, probably the greatest man now living, whose extraordinary abilities we of the Weapon Shops are just beginning to appreciate. I am referring to Robert Hedrock, who holds the rank of Captain in Your Majesty's army."

To Gonish's amazement, the Empress leaned toward him. Her gaze was intense, her lips parted breathlessly, her eyes shining.

"You mean," she whispered, "the Weapon Shops consider Robert—Captain Hedrock—as one of the world's great men?" She did not wait for a reply, but turned to Prince del Curtin. "You see," she said. *"You see!"*

The prince smiled. "Your Majesty," he said quietly, "my opinion of Captain Hedrock has always been high."

The woman faced Gonish across the table, said in a strangely formal tone, "I will see to it that Captain Hedrock is advised of your urgent desire to interview him."

She knew! He had that much. As for the rest—Gonish leaned back in his chair ruefully. She would advise Hedrock, would she? He could just imagine Hedrock's sardonic reception of the information. Gonish straightened slowly. His situation was becoming desperate. The entire Weapon Shop world was geared to act on the results of this meeting. And still he had nothing.

There was no doubt that these people were as anxious to get rid of the giant as the Weapon Makers were to get hold of Hedrock; and the irony was that the death of Hedrock would simultaneously solve both problems. With an effort, Gonish mustered his best smile, and said, "You seem to have a little mystery among yourselves about Captain Hedrock. May I ask what it is?"

Surprisingly, the question brought a puzzled stare from Prince del Curtin. "I should have thought," the man said finally, politely, "that in your fashion you would long ago have put two and two together. Or is it possible that, of all the people of the solar system, you are not aware of what happened tonight. Where have you been since 7:45?"

Gonish was startled. In his desire to keep his mind clear for this meeting, he had come early to Imperial City. At 7:30 he had gone into a quiet little restaurant. Emerging an hour and a half later, he had attended a play. That ended at 11:53. Since then, he had wandered along sight-seeing. He had ignored the news. He knew nothing. Incredibly, half the world could have been destroyed and he wouldn't know. Prince del Curtin was speaking again:

"It is true that the identity of the man in such a case is traditionally withheld, but—"

"Prince!"

It was the Empress, her voice low and tense. The men looked at her, startled, as she went on, more grimly, "Say no more. There is something wrong. All this questioning about Captain Hedrock has an ulterior motive. They're only partly interested in the giant."

She herself must have realized that her warning was too late. She stopped and looked at Gonish, and the look in her eyes brought pity welling up in him. Until this moment, he had never regarded the Empress Isher as quite human. But there could be no pity. With a jerk, Gonish brought his hand up near his mouth, tore back the sleeve, and said ringingly into the tiny radio that was strapped there:

"Captain Hedrock is in the Empress' personal apartment—"

They were quick, those three men. They bowled him over in one concerted rush; and then they were on top of him. Gonish offered no resistance, but submitted quietly to arrest. After a moment, he felt relief that he, who had been compelled by inexorable duty to betray his friend, would now die, too.

15

THE RUINS CONSISTED OF A BREAKTHROUGH INTO A MAIN corridor of the palace, and of gaping energy holes along the corridor itself where the fighting had taken place.

Beside the Empress, Prince del Curtin said anxiously, "Hadn't you better get some sleep, Your Majesty? It's after four. And, as the Weapon Makers have not answered our repeated calls, there is nothing more that can be done tonight about your husband . . . about Captain Hedrock."

She waved him away, vaguely. There was a thought in her mind, a thought so sharp that it seemed to have physical qualities; so painful that every moment it existed it was a bit of hell. She must get him back; no matter what the sacrifice, she must have Hedrock back. Strange, she thought finally, how she who had been so cold and steely and calculating, so almost inhumanly imperial—strange how in the ultimate issue she should prove to be like all the women who had ever become emotional over a man. As if the first shock of committing herself to one man had literally changed the chemistry of her body. When Hedrock had been announced at six o'clock the night before, her mind was already made up. She thought of her decision as intellectual, product of the need for an Isher heir. Actually, of course, she had never thought of anyone but Hedrock as the father. In the first audience she had granted him eight months earlier, he had coolly announced that he had come to the palace for the sole purpose of marrying her. That amused, then angered, then enraged her, but it had put him in the special category as the only man who had ever asked for her hand. The psychology involved had always been plain; and she sometimes felt acutely the unfairness of the situation for other men who might have the ambition or desire. Court etiquette forbade that they mention the subject. The tradition was that she must ask. She never had.

In the final issue she had thought only of the man who had actually proposed; and, at six o'clock he had come in response to her urgent call and agreed instantly to an immediate marriage. The ceremony had been simple but public. Public in that she took her vows before the telestat, so that all the world might see her and hear her words. Hedrock had not appeared on the telestat. His name was not mentioned. He was referred to as "the distinguished officer who has won Her Majesty's esteem." He was a consort only, and as such must remain in the background.

Only the Ishers mattered. The men and women they married remained private persons. That was the law; and she had never thought there was anything wrong with it. She didn't now, but for nearly ten hours she had been a wife, and during those hours her mind and metabolism adjusted. The thoughts that came had no relation to any she had ever had before. Curious thoughts about how she must now bear the chosen man's children, and mother them, and of how the palace must be transformed spiritually so that children could live there. After six hours she had told him of her appointment to meet Edward Gonish. And went off with the memory of the odd expression in his eyes—and now this ruin, and the gathering realization that Hedrock was gone, snatched irresistibly from the heart of her empire by her old enemies. She grew aware that someone, the court chancellor, was recounting a list of precautions that had been taken to prevent leakage of the news that the palace had been attacked.

No reports had been permitted to be broadcast. Every witness was being sworn to silence under strict penalties. By

107

dawn, the repair work would be completed without trace, and thereafter any story that did come out would seem a bare-faced rumor, to be laughed at, and ridiculed. It had been, she realized, fast, effective suppression. Very important, that. The prestige of the House of Isher might have been dealt a damaging blow. But the success of the censorship made it all remote, secondary. There would be rewards and honors to dole out, but what mattered now was, she must get him back.

Slowly, she emerged from her dark mood. Her party, she saw, was clear now of the muttering repair machines, and was moving along the wrecked corridor. Her mind withdrew further from itself, grew more intent on her surroundings. She thought: the important thing was to find out what had happened, then act. Frowning from her new purpose, she examined the mutilated walls of the hallway. Her green eyes flashed. She said with a semblance of her old sardonicism, "From the slant of the ray burns, our side seems to have done all the damage, except for the initial breach in the main wall."

One of the officers nodded grimly. "They were after Captain Hedrock only. They used a peculiar paralysing ray that toppled our soldiers over like ninepins. The men are still recovering with no harmful effects visible, much as General Grall did after Captain Hedrock seemed to cause him to die from heart failure at lunch two months ago."

"But what happened?" she demanded sharply. "Bring me someone who saw everything. Was Captain Hedrock asleep when the attack came?"

"No—" The officer spoke cautiously. "No, Your Majesty, he was down in the tombs."

"Where?"

The soldier looked unhappy. "Your Majesty, as soon as you and your party left the palace, Captain Hed . . . your consor—"

She said impatiently, "Call him Prince Hedrock, please."

"Thank you, Majesty. Prince Hedrock went down in the tombs to one of the old storerooms, removed part of one wall—"

"He what? But go on!"

"Yes, Your Majesty. Naturally, in view of his new position, our guards gave him every assistance in removing the section of metal wall and transporting it to the elevators, and up to this corridor."

"Naturally."

"The soldiers who reported to me said the wall section was weightless but it offered some quality of innate resistance to movement. It was about two feet wide and six and a half feet long; and when Cap . . . Prince Hedrock stepped through it and

108

vanished, and then came back, it—"

"When he what? Colonel, what are you talking about?"

The officer bowed. "I regret my confusion, Madame. I did not see all of this, but I have pieced together varied accounts. My mind of course persists in regarding as more important what I myself saw. I actually saw him enter the detached wall shield, disappear, and return a minute later."

The Empress stood there, her mind almost a blank. She knew she would get the story eventually, but right now it seemed beyond her reach, buried deep in a muddle of phrases that had no meaning in themselves. Captain Hedrock had gone to the tombs deep below the palace, removed a section of wall, and then what?

She put the question incisively; and the colonel said, "And then, Your Majesty, he brought it up to the palace proper and stood waiting."

"This was before the attack?"

The officer shook his head. "During it. He was still in the tombs when the wall was breached by the concentrated fire of the Weapon Shop warships. I warned him personally in my capacity of chief of the palace guards of what was happening. The warning only made him speed his return to the surface, where he was captured."

Briefly again she felt helpless. The description seemed clear enough now. But it made no sense. Hedrock must have known something was going to happen, because he had gone purposely down into the tombs immediately after her own departure to meet Edward Gonish. That part was all right. It seemed to indicate a plan. The strange thing was that he had come up and, right before the eyes of the Weapon Shop forces and the palace guards, had apparently used the wall section to transmit himself somewhere, as the Weapon Makers were reputed to be able to do. But, instead of staying away, he had come back. Insanely, he had come back, and permitted the Weapon Makers to take him prisoner.

She said finally, hopelessly, "What happened to the section of wall?"

"It burned up right after Prince Hedrock warned the Weapon Shop councilor, Peter Cadron, who led the attackers."

"Warned—" She turned to del Curtin. "Prince, perhaps you can obtain a coherent story. I'm lost."

The prince said quietly, "We're all tired, Your Majesty. Colonel Nison has been up all night." He turned to the flushing officer. "Colonel, as I understand it, guns from Weapon Shop warships breached the gap in the outer wall at the end of the corridor. Then one of the ships drew alongside, and sent men into the corridor, men who were immune to the fire of our troops—is that right?"

"Absolutely, sir."

"They were led by Peter Cadron of the Weapon Makers' Council, and when they reached a certain point in the corridor, there was Prince Hedrock standing waiting. He had brought some kind of electronic plate or shield, six feet by two feet, from a hiding-place in the tombs. He stood beside it, waited until everybody could see his action, then stepped *into* the plate, vanishing as he did so.

"The plate continued to stand there, apparently held in place from the other side; this would account for the resistance it offered when the soldiers carried it up from the tombs for Prince Hedrock. A minute after his disappearance, Prince Hedrock stepped back out of the shield and, facing the Weapon Shop men, warned Peter Cadron."

"That is correct, sir."

"What was the warning?"

The officer said steadily, "He asked Councilor Cadron if he recalled the Weapon Shop laws forbidding any interference, for any reason, with the seat of Imperial Government, and warned him that the entire Weapon Shop Council would regret its high-handed action, and that it would be taught to remember that it is but one of two facets of Isher civilization."

"He said *that*!" Her voice was eager, her eyes ablaze. She whirled on del Curtin. "Prince, did you hear that?"

The prince bowed, then turned back to Colonel Nison.

"My last question is this: In your opinion did Prince Hedrock give any evidence of being able to fulfil his threat against the Weapon Makers?"

"None, sir. I could have shot him myself from where I stood. Physically he was, and I presume it, completely in their power."

"Thank you," said the prince. "That is all."

There remained the fact that she must rescue Captain Hedrock. She paced up and down, up and down. Dawn came, a gray muggy light that peered through the huge windows of her office apartment shedding vague pools of light in its shadowy corners, and making no impression at all where there were artificial lights. She saw that Prince del Curtin was watching her anxiously. She slowed her rapid pacing, and said, "I can't believe it. I can't believe that Captain Hedrock would say things out of bravado. It is possible that there exists some organization of which we know nothing. In fact—" She faced him wildly. "Prince," she said in an intense voice, "he *told* me that he was not, never had been, never would be a Weapon Shop man."

Del Curtin was frowning. "Innelda," he said pityingly, "you

110

are exciting yourself uselessly. There can't be anything. Human beings, being what they are, sooner or later manifest any power they may have. That is a law as fixed as Einsteinian gravitation. If such an organization existed, we would have known of it."

"We have missed the clues. Don't you see?" Her voice trembled with the desperation of her thought. "He came to marry me. And he won there. That shows the calibre of the organization. And what about the section of wall that he removed from the store-room in the tombs—how did that get there? Explain that."

"Surely," said the prince in a stately voice, "the Ishers cannot but be mortal enemies of any secret organization that may exist!"

"The Ishers," said the woman icily, "are learning that they are human beings as well as rulers, and that the world is a big place, too big for one mind or group of minds to comprehend in its entirety."

They stared at each other, two people whose nerves were frayed to the utmost. It was the Empress who recovered first. She said wearily, "It seems incredible, Prince, that you and I who have been almost truly brother and sister, should be on the verge of a quarrel. I'm sorry."

She came forward and placed her hand on his. He took it and kissed it. There were tears in his eyes as he straightened. "Your Majesty," he said huskily, "I beg your forgiveness. I should have remembered the strain you are undergoing. You have but to command me. We have power. A billion men will spring to arms at your command. We can threaten the Weapon Makers with a generation of war. We can destroy any man who has dealings with them. We can—"

She shook her head hopelessly. "My dear, you do not realize what you are saying. This is an age that would normally be revolutionary. The necessary disorganized mental outlook exists. The evils are there: selfish administration, corrupt courts, and rapacious industry. Every class contributes its own brand of amoral and immoral attributes, which are beyond the control of any individual. Life itself is in the driver's seat; we are only passengers. So far our marvellous science, the immensity of machine production, the intricate and superb organization of law, and"—she hesitated, then went on reluctantly—"the existence of the Weapon Makers as a stabilizing influence, have prevented an open explosion. But for a generation at least, we mustn't rock the boat. I am counting particularly upon a new method of mind training recently released by the Weapon Shops, which strengthens moral function as well as performing everything that other methods are noted for. As soon as we get rid of the menace of the giant organization we—"

She stopped because of the startled expression that flashed into the prince's lean face. Her eyes widened. She whispered, "It's impossible. He ... can't be ... the giant. Wait ... Wait, don't do anything. We can prove it all in a minute—"

She crossed swiftly to her personal 'stat, said in a tired, flat voice, "Bring the prisoner, Edward Gonish, to my office."

For five minutes she stood almost unmoving until the door opened and Gonish was ushered in. The guards departed on her command. She relaxed sufficiently then to ask the questions.

The No-man answered her steadily. "I do not understand the electronic shield through which you say he disappeared, but yes, Your Majesty, Captain Hedrock is one of the giants, or"—he hesitated, then added slowly—"or, and this thought has just come, *the* giant."

The significance of the hesitation was not lost on her. She swayed wearily. "But why should he want to marry the woman whose empire he is trying to ruin?"

"Madam"—Gonish spoke quietly—"it was only two months ago that we discovered Captain Hedrock was deceiving the Weapon Shops. It was the accidental disclosure of his remarkably superior intelligence that proved him to be a man to whom the Isher line and the Weapon Makers are but a means to an end. What that end is, I am only beginning to suspect. If you will answer a few questions, I shall be able to tell you in a few minutes who Captain Hedrock is, or rather, was! I say 'was' of necessity. I regret to say that the intention of the Weapon Makers was to question him in a specially constructed chamber; then immediately execute him."

Silence settled over the room. Actually, the capacity of her body for shock was gone. She stood, cold and numb, without thought, waiting. She noticed finally, absently, that the No-man was an extremely distinguished-looking individual. She studied him, and then forgot his personal appearance as he began to speak:

"I have, of course, all the information about Captain Hedrock that is known to the Weapon Makers. My search led into very unusual by-ways. But if similar curious paths exist in the Isher annals, as I believe they do, then the section of wall Hedrock removed from the tombs is only the final clue. But let me ask: Is there any picture, or film, *any* physical record available of the husband of the Empress Ganeel?"

"Why—no!" The breathlessness was accompanied by a dizziness, almost a spinning of her brain for her mind had made

112

an improbable leap. She spoke blurrily, "Mr. Gonish, he said that, except for my dark hair, I reminded him of Ganeel."

The No-man bowed gravely. "Your Majesty, I see you have already plunged into these strange waters. I want you to run your mind back and *back* through the history of your line, and remember—whose pictorial record is missing, husband or emperor?"

"They're mostly husbands of empresses," she said slowly, steadily. "That is how the traditions began, that consorts should remain in the background." She frowned. "So far as I know there is only one emperor, of whom picture, portrait or film record is not available. That one is understandable. As the first of the line, he—"

She stopped. She stared at Gonish. "Are you crazy?" she said. "Are you *crazy*?"

The No-man shook his head. "You may now regard it as a full intuition. You know what my training is. I take a fact here and a fact there, and as soon as I have approximately ten per cent, the answer comes automatically. They call it intuition, but actually it is simply the ability of the brain to co-ordinate tens of thousands of facts in a flash, and to logicalize any gaps that may exist.

"One of the facts in this case is that there are no less than twenty-seven important pictorial records missing in the history of the Weapon Shops. I concentrated my attention on the writing of the men in question, and the similarity of mental outlook, the breadth of intellect, was unmistakable." He finished. "You may or may not know it, but just as the first and greatest of the Ishers is only a name, so our founder, Walter S. de Lany, is a name without a face."

"But who is he?" said Prince del Curtin, blankly. "Apparently, somewhere along the line the race of man bred an immortal."

"Not bred. It must have been artificial. Had it been natural, it would have been repeated many times in these centuries. And it must have been accidental, and unrepeatable, because everything the man has ever said or done shows an immense and passionate interest in the welfare of the race.'

"But," said the prince, "what is he trying to do? Why did he marry Innelda?"

For a moment, Gonish was silent. He stared at the woman, and she returned his gaze, the colour in her cheeks high and brilliant. Finally she nodded, and Gonish said:

"For one thing, he has tried to keep the Isher strain *Isher*. He believes in his own blood, and rightly so, as history has proven. For instance, you two are only remotely Isher. Your blood is so diluted that your kinship to Captain Hedrock can

113

hardly be called a relation. Hedrock remarked to me once that the Isher emperors tended to marry brilliant and somewhat unstable women, and that this periodically endangered the family. It was the empresses, he said, who always saved the line by marrying steady, sober, able men."

"Suppose—" The woman did not think of her words as an interruption; the thought came; she spoke it. "Suppose we offered to trade you for him?"

Gonish shrugged. "You can probably obtain his corpse for me."

That burned and chilled by turns, but the brief fever left her colder, more remote from emotion. Death was something that she had seen with icy eyes, and she could face it for *him* as well as for herself.

"Suppose I were to offer the interstellar drive?"

Her intensity seemed to astound the man. He drew back and stared at her. "Madam," he said finally, "I can offer you no intuition one way or the other, nor any logical hope. I must admit that I am puzzled by the electronic shield, but I get nothing, no sense of what it could be, or why it should help him. Whatever he did when he was *within* it could not to my knowledge assist him to escape through the impregnable walls of a Weapon Shop battle cruiser, or out of the metal room where he was taken. All the science of the Weapon Makers and the Isher Empire is arrayed against him. Science moves in spurts, and we are in the dynamic middle of the latest one. A hundred years from now, when the lull has set in, an immortal man may begin to get his bearings, not before."

"Suppose he tells them the truth?" It was Prince del Curtin who spoke.

"Never!" the woman flashed. "Why, that would be begging. No Isher would think of such a thing."

Gonish said, "Her Majesty is right, but that is not the only reason. I will not explain. The possibility of a confession does not exist."

She was only vaguely aware of his words. She whirled on her cousin. She held herself straight, her head high. She said in a thrillingly clear voice, "Keep trying to contact the Weapon Makers. Offer them Gonish, the interstellar drive, and legal recognition, including an arrangement whereby their courts and ours establish a liaison, all in exchange for Captain Hedrock. They would be mad to refuse."

The passion sagged. She saw that the No-man was gazing at her gloomily. "Madam," he said sadly, "you have obviously paid no attention to my earlier statement. The intention was to kill him within a maximum of one hour. In view of his previous escape from the Weapon Makers, that intention will

114

not be deviated from. The greatest human story in history is over. And, Madam—"

The No-man stared at her steadily. "For your sake, it is just as well. You know as well as I do that you cannot have children."

"What's this?" said Prince del Curtin in a vast amazement. "Innelda—"

"Silence!" Her voice was harsh with mortified fury. "Prince, have this man returned to his cell. He has really become intolerable. And I forbid you to discuss your sovereign with him."

The prince bowed. "Your Majesty commands," he said coldly. He turned. "This way, Mr. Gonish."

She had wondered if she could be hurt further; and here it was. She stood, after a moment, alone in her shattered world. Long minutes dragged before she realized that sleep at least would be kind.

16

IT WAS NOT SO MUCH A ROOM IN WHICH HEDROCK FOUND himself as a metal cavern. He stopped short in the doorway, beside Peter Cadron, a sardonic smile on his face. He saw that the councilor was watching him from narrowed eyes, and his lips curled.

Let them wonder and doubt. They had surprised him once by an unexpected arrest. This time it was different. This time he was ready for them. His gaze played boldly over the twenty-nine men who sat around the V table which the Weapon Maker Council used in their public hearings. He waited until Peter Cadron, the thirtieth of that high council, had walked over and seated himself; waited while the commander of the guards reported that the prisoner was stripped of all rings, that his clothes had been changed and his body subjected to a transparency and found to be normal, with nowhere a hidden weapon.

Having spoken, the commander and his guards withdrew, but still Hedrock waited. He smiled as Peter Cadron explained the reason for the precautions; and then, slowly, coolly, he walked forward and faced the open end of the V table. He saw that the men's eyes were on him. Some looked curious, some expectant, some merely hostile. All seemed willing for him to speak.

"Gentlemen," Hedrock said in his ringing voice, "I'm going to ask one question: Does anyone present know where I was when I stepped through that shield? If not, I would suggest that I be released at once because the mighty Weapon Makers' Council is in for a devil of a shock."

There was silence. The men looked at each other. "I would say," said young Ancil Nare, "that the sooner the execution is carried out the better. At the present moment, his throat can but cut; he can be strangled; a bullet can smash his head; an energy gun disintegrate him. His body is without protection— if necessary we could even club him to death. We know that all this can be done *this instant*. We do not know, in view of his strange statements, that it can be done ten minutes from now." In his earnestness, the youthful executive stood up as he finished, "Gentlemen, let us act now!"

Hedrock's loud clapping broke the silence that followed. "Bravo," he said, "bravo. Such well-spoken advice merits being acted upon. Go ahead and try to kill me in any fashion you please. Draw your guns and fire; pick up your chairs and bludgeon me; order knives and pin me against the wall. No matter what you do, gentlemen, you're in for a shock." His eyes were chilling. "And deservedly so.

"Wait!" His thunderous voice crowned the attempt of the solid-faced Deam Lealy to break into speech. "*I'll* do the talking. It is the Council that is on trial, not I. It can still win leniency for its criminal action in attacking the Imperial Palace by recognizing now, without further offence, that it has broken its own laws."

"Really," a councilor wedged in the words, "this is beyond toleration."

"Let him talk," Peter Cadron said. "We shall learn a great deal about his motives."

Hedrock bowed gravely. "Indeed you shall, Mr. Cadron. My motives are concerned entirely with the action of this Council in ordering the attack on the palace."

"I can understand," said Cadron ironically, "your vexation that this Council did not respect a regulation more than three thousand years old when apparently you had counted upon it and upon our natural reluctance to make such an attack, and accordingly felt yourself safe to pursue your own ends, whatever they are."

Hedrock said steadily, "I did *not* count upon the regulation or the reluctance. My colleagues and I"—it was just as well to suggest once more that he was not alone—"have noted with regret the developing arrogance of this Council, its growing belief that it was not accountable for its actions, and that

116

therefore it could safely flout its own constitution."

"Our constitution," said Bayd Roberts, the senior councilor, with dignity, "demands that we take any action necessary to maintain our position. The proviso that this be done without an attack on the person or residence of the reigning Isher, her heirs or successors, has no meaning in an extreme emergency such as this. You will notice that we did secure the absence of Her Majesty during the attack."

"I must interrupt." It was the chairman of the Council. "Incredibly, the prisoner had succeeded in concentrating the conversation according to his own desires. I can understand that we all have a guilty feeling about the attack on the palace, but we are not required to defend our actions to the prisoner." He spoke curtly into his chair-arm 'stat, "Commander, come in here and put a sack over the prisoner's head."

Hedrock was smiling gently as the guard of ten came in. He said, "We will now have the shock."

He stood perfectly still as the men grabbed him. The sack came up and—

It happened.

When Hedrock, in the palace half an hour before, had stepped through the section of wall which he had brought up from the tombs, he found himself in a dim world. He stood for a long time letting his body adjust, hoping that no one would attempt to follow him through that electronic-force field. It was not a personal worry. The vibratory shield was tuned to his body and his alone and during all the years that it had been part of the wall in the underground palace storeroom, the only danger had been that someone might unknowingly wander into it, and suffer damage. Hedrock had often wondered what would happen to such an unlucky innocent. Several animals that he had tagged and put through an experimental model had been sent back from points as far away as ten thousand miles. Some had never been returned despite the high reward offer printed on the tag.

Now that he himself was in, there was no hurry. Normal time and space laws had no meaning in this realm of half-light. It was nowhere and it was everywhere. It was the quickest place in which to go mad, because the body that intruded on it experienced time; *it* didn't. He had found that a six-hour session made serious inroads on his sanity. His incursion earlier in the evening, through the shield in his hide-out, had been for what would have been two hours normal time, and the trip had revealed to him that the Empress wanted to marry him. Temporarily, that had guaranteed his safety; what was more important, it also guaranteed he would have access to the shield in the palace tombs. Accordingly, he had withdrawn swiftly, conserving the remaining four hours of the six that was the human limit.

His present incursion mustn't occupy more than four hours, preferably three, more preferably two. After which, he'd have to stay away from the mind-destroying thing for months. The idea for the invention had been broached to him during one of his terms as chairman of the Weapon Makers' Council, an enormously autocratic position that had enabled him to assign an entire laboratory of physicists to assist the brilliant young man whose brain child it was. Simply, the problem had been: The Weapon Shop vibratory transmitter bridged the spatial gap between two points in interplanetary space by mechanically accepting that space had no material existence. Why not then, the inventor had expounded, why not reverse the process and create an illusion of space where there had been nothing?

The research was a success. The inventor reported the details to Hedrock, who thought it over and informed the man and his colleagues that the Council had decided on secrecy. To the Council itself, he made a negative report on the invention. And it had. The subject, once explored, was considered one more closed door, was entered as such in the files of Information Center for the future reference of men who might have a repetition of the idea. Accordingly, it would never again be the subject of Weapon Shop research. Some day, he would release the knowledge.

It was, Hedrock reflected, as he stood there patiently letting his body adjust, not the first time that an invention had come into his possession and been withheld from the public. His own discovery, vibratory magnification, he had kept as a personal secret for twenty centuries before finally using it to established the Weapon Shops as a counter-balance to the Isher emperors. He still had several others. And his main rule for withholding or not had always been: Would release for general use be of benefit to the progressive spirit of man? Or would the power that it represented merely assist some temporal group in tightening a tyranny already too rigid? Quite enough dangerous inventions were carelessly produced during the inventive spurts that came every few centuries by scientists who never thought in a practical fashion of what the effect of their discoveries might be.

Damn it, why should a billion people die because some inventor had a brain that couldn't see an inch into human nature?

Then, of course, there were the people who saw an invention in terms of their own private or group welfare. If they were withholding, as the Empress was withholding the inter-

118

stellar drive, they must be forced by all means to yield their secret. Sometimes, the decision had been a hard one, but who else had the power, the experience to decide? For better or for worse, he was the arbiter.

He let the thought drain slowly out of him. His body was ready. The time had come for action. Hedrock began to walk forward in the mist. He could see the people in the palace, standing rigidly like carved figures seen at late dusk. His time relation to them had not changed a single instant. He paid them no attention, even when they were in his way, but stepped through their bodies as if they were clouds of gas. Walls yielded before his mass, but that had to be carefully done. It would have been just as easy, too easy, to sink through the floor, and so on into the earth. The laboratory experiments of the inventor and his assistants had produced one such casualty; and repetition was not desired. To avoid the calamity, the research staff finally designed that the initial creation of new space should be on a partial scale only. A ring was provided which, when activated, would increase or decrease the original apportionment at will, for use when heavy materials had to be penetrated.

The ring, one of two—the other had a different purpose—was what Hedrock used when he came to walls. First, an easy jump, followed as his feet left the floor by a touch on the activator of the ring, then swift release of the activator, and then a gentle landing on a floor that gave like thick mud under his feet. It was simple for muscles so perfectly co-ordinated as his own. He reached the cache of machines which he had long ago tuned to this space, and secreted in the palace. There was a small spaceship, with lifting devices, magnetizers large and small, particularly there were dozens of machines that could snatch and hold things. There were various weapons and, of course, every tool, every instrument from spaceship to mechanical fingers had its own equivalent of the two adjusters necessary to their complete operation. Every instrument in the ship, the ship itself, and the two adjuster rings on Hedrock's finger, were attuned to a master control on the switchboard of the spaceship.

The second ring and the matching adjusters on the machine comprised the second valuable function of the invention. By controlling the second ring, it was possible to go backward and forward in time for a short distance. Theoretically, years could be covered; actually, the shattering effect of the entire experience to the human brain limited a trip to a few hours backward or forward.

Hedrock had discovered that, in nine hours forward in time, and nine backward, eighteen altogether, the body lived the six normal hours that it could endure without going too insane. Three for one. The method of time travel had no relation to the seesaw system of time travel unwittingly devised by the Empress' physicists seven years before, wherein the body collected time energy which could never again quite be balanced off, with the result that the time traveler was always destroyed. There was no time in *this* space; there was only a method of adjusting the space to a given time in the normal world.

Hedrock eased the little spaceship and everything in it around to where the Weapon Shop cruiser lay-to beside the break in the palace wall. Through the hard shell of the cruiser, he nosed his machine; then switched off the engines, and turned on the master time adjuster to full power, thrice the rate of normal time. He waited tensely, watching the Sensitives, which were nothing but automatic relays converted to use in this space. It shouldn't take long. The Sensitive lights flashed; the master switch clicked instantly down to one-third its full power, adjusting the whole ship to normal-time rate. Simultaneously, Hedrock felt movement. The great Weapon Shop cruiser was rising; and he and his small machine were with it, perfectly matched as to time rate, and just far enough out of the special space to keep from falling through the walls of the cruiser.

If he was right, there were now two Hedrocks in the cruiser, himself here in the gray-dark realm, and himself returned to the palace *from* this very spy trip, made prisoner by the Weapon Makers and brought aboard the cruiser. It was unwise to take that for granted. One of the difficulties of moving around in time was that of locating people, and keeping track of them in crowds, or just keeping track. He had once wasted an entire six-hour period searching for a person who had gone to a theatre. Accordingly, even now, it was best to make sure. He peered into the 'stats; and, yes, there he was, surrounded by guards. The Hedrock out there was already back from this time trip, and knew what had happened. Which was more than *he* did. It shouldn't take long, though.

The cruiser flashed to the fortress that was its destination. Prisoner and guards emerged and went down into the building, where the thick metal room had been constructed. Hedrock forced his ship through the heavy walls and got busy. First, he put out a sound collector; and while listening to the argument in the room, unloaded some of his machines. When the guards rushed in with the "sack", which was simply a gagging device, he waited till it was about to be fastened, then lowered a mechanical hand and snatched it into his own space. He sat then, with his fingers on the time control, waiting for developments.

In the room itself, the silence was a thing of tensed nerves and startled looks. Hedrock, the prisoner, stood still, a faint, sardonic smile on his lips, making no effort to break the grip of the guards who held him. He felt remorseless. There was a job to be done, and he intended to do it thoroughly. He said icily, "I won't waste any time on verbal argument. The determination of this organization to kill me, despite the fact that the Pp machine proved my altruism and good will shows a defensive conservatism that always tries to destroy when confronted by something it does not completely understand. That conservatism shall be taught by overwhelming force that there exists an organization capable of overthrowing even the mighty Weapon Makers."

Peter Cadron said coldly, "The Weapon Shops recognize no secret organization. Guards, destroy him!"

"You fool," Hedrock cried. "I thought better of you, Cadron, than that you would give such a command after what I have said."

He went on talking, paying no attention to what was happening. Without looking around at the guards, he *knew*.

In that other space, his earlier self simply cut the time-adjuster switch, whereupon everything in the room stabilized. Without haste, his earlier self relieved the guards of their weapons, and then proceeded to disarm every member of the Council including the removal of the rings from their fingers and the 'stat radios from their wrists and chairs. Next, he slipped handcuffs on to their wrists, chaining them all together in a long row around the table. The guards he handcuffed arms to legs, and set outside in the hallway. Then he closed and locked the door. The whole job took no time. Literally.

He returned to the control board, adjusted his time rate from zero to normal and listened to the uproar of the men discovering their situation.

The dismay was vast. Chains clanked. Men cried out in wonder and alarm, and then sank back looking pale and terrified. Hedrock knew there was very little personal fear involved. It was all too plain that every man present had suddenly had a terrible vision of the end of the Weapon Shops.

He waited for their startled attention to jerk back to him, then spoke swiftly, "Gentlemen, calm your fears. Your great organization is not in danger. This situation would never have arisen if you had not pursued me with such singleness of purpose. For your information, it was your own founder, Walter S. de Lany, who recognized the danger to the State of an invincible body such as the Weapon Makers. It was he who set a

121

group of friendly watchers over the Shops. That is all I will say, except to emphasize our friendliness, our good will, our resolve not to interfere so long as the Weapon Makers live according to their Constitution. It is that Constitution which has now been violated in its one inflexible article."

He paused there, his gaze sweeping the faces before him, but mentally he was coolly appraising his words. It was a good story withal, the lack of detail being its safest feature. All he desired from it was that it conceal the fact that an immortal man was the only watcher. He saw that several of the men had recovered sufficiently to attempt speech, but he cut them off.

"Here is what must be done. First, keep silent about what you have learned today. The Watchers do not wish it known that they exist. Secondly, resign *in toto*. You can all stand for re-election, not for the next term, but thereafter. The mass resignation will serve as a reminder to the rank and file of the Shops that there is a Constitution and that it is one to respect. Finally, no further attempt to molest me must be made. About noon tomorrow, inform the Empress that you have released me, and ask her to give up the interstellar drive. I think myself that the drive will be forthcoming before that hour without any urging, but give her the chance to be generous."

His voice must have been holding them in thrall. As he finished, there was an angry clamor, then silence, and then a lesser clamor, and silence again. Hedrock did not fail to notice that three or four men, among them Peter Cadron, did not join in either manifestation of that confusion. It was to Cadron that Hedrock addressed himself, "I am sure that Mr. Cadron can act as spokesman. I have long regarded him as one of the most able members on the Council."

Cadron climbed to his feet, a strongly-built man in his middle forties. "Yes," he said, "I believe I can be spokesman. I think I speak for the majority when I say that we accept your terms."

No one dissented. Hedrock bowed and said loudly, "All right, No. 1, pull me out!"

He must have vanished instantly.

They attempted no experiments, the two Hedrocks who were briefly together in that misty partial space. The human brain suffered too greatly from the slightest interference with time. Numerous tests had proved that fact long before. The "earlier" Hedrock sat at the controls of the little ship, driving it hard back in time and toward the palace. The other stood beside him, looking down gloomily.

He had done what he could. As a result the psychological direction events were taking was so marked that the issue was no longer in doubt. It was possible that Innelda would hold the interstellar drive back for bargaining purposes. But that didn't matter. Victory was sure.

The trouble was that greater beings had "freed" him to see what he would do. Somewhere out in space a vast fleet manned by a spider race had paused to study man and his actions. Having captured him they had instantly traced him back to his planet of origin, and manipulated him as if distance did not exist. Having watched him carry out his original purpose, and realizing that there would be little point in further observation of a person who had completed an action, they would undoubtedly reassert control of him.

Theoretically they might now be bored with human beings, and destroy the solar system and all its intensely emotional inhabitants. Such destruction would be a mere incident in their coldly intellectual existence.

With a grimace, as he reached that point in his thought, Hedrock saw that they were at their destination. The shield loomed up in the dim reaches of the shadowy palace, a rectangular shape of soft brilliance. The two Hedrocks tried no trickery, attempted no paradox. It was his "earlier" self who stepped through the shield and became one more misty form in the palace room. Hedrock sprayed the combustible shield with a sticky explosive powder, and set it afire. He waited till it had burned, and then he sent the little ship hurtling across the dark city toward one of his dozen secret apartments. Swiftly, he set the Sensitives to hold the ship at normal time rate for possible future use, then he focused the power of the lifter on himself, and felt it lower him into the apartment.

The moment he was on his feet, he headed for a comfortable armchair. When he had settled himself, he called in a savage tone, "All right, my spider friends, if you have any further plans, better try to carry them out now."

The greater struggle had still to be made.

17

HIS FIRST AWARENESS OF THE PRESENCE OF THE ALIENS WAS a thought, not directed at him, but which was intended for him to understand. The thought was on the old titanic level, so violent that his brain was shocked by the impact:

"—AN INTERESTING EXAMPLE OF AN ENERGY IMPULSE CONTINUING AS IF NO OUTSIDE FORCE

HAD BEEN APPLIED—"

"NO!" The answer was cold. "THE MAN WAS AWARE OF US. THE PURPOSE DRIVING HIM WAS CARRIED THROUGH IN SPITE OF HIS KNOWLEDGE OF OUR EXISTENCE."

"CLEARLY, THEN, HE ACTED ILLOGICALLY."

"POSSIBLY. BUT LET US BRING HIM BACK. . . . HERE . . ."

Hedrock recognized that the critical moment had come. For many hours he had been thinking of what he would do when it arrived, and for more than a minute, ever since he had sat down, he had been doing it.

His eyes were closed, his body calm, his mind slow and blank. It was not a perfect state of what the ancient Hindu fakirs had called Nirvana but it was a condition of profound relaxation; and millenia before, the great institutes for mind and sensory study had used it as the basis for all mind training. Sitting there, Hedrock grew conscious of a steady and enormous pulsing that shook his brain with its thunder. But that physical phase, that pounding of his heart with its attendant murmurs of blood flow, and all the tens of thousands of muscular tensions each with its own tiny sounds—that phase, also, passed. He was alone with utter calm and utter peace.

His first impression, then, was that he was sitting in a chair —but not the chair of his apartment. The picture grew so clear that he knew after a few seconds that the chair was in the control room of the lifeboat which in turn was inside one of the huge alien-controlled spaceships.

Hedrock sighed, and opened his eyes. He sat there letting the familiarity of the surroundings figuratively suffuse his being. So his resistance had failed. It was too bad, but of course he had not positively counted on success. He continued to sit in the multi-purposed control chair, because relaxation was his only method of resistance; and he intended to resist from now on.

While he waited, he glanced lazily into the glowing 'stats. Three of the view plates showed starry space, but there was an image of a ship in the rear view plate. Odd, he thought. His lifeboat must no longer be inside the alien machine. He considered that with a faint frown, and then he noticed something else. There was only one ship. But, then, where were the hundreds of others?

He fought down a rising excitement, as he realized what was happening. The relaxation process was working. *Had* worked to some extent. The spider beings had succeeded in bringing him back to his lifeboat, but their domination of his mind was partially broken; and so several of their illusions had faded from his mind.

The first illusion had been that there was more than one ship. Now, free of their control, he could see that there was only one. The second illusion had been that his lifeboat had been inside their machine. Now, free of their control, he could see that it wasn't. He was about to go on in that orderly fashion when his mind leaped to the possibility that their control of him was probably very tenuous at this moment. He closed his eyes, and he was about to think himself back to his apartment when there was an interruption.

"Man, do not compel us to destroy you."

He had been expecting a mental interference, instinctively cringing in anticipation of the titanic impact of it. The shock was different from his expectation. The alien thought lacked force. It seemed far away, weak. Hedrock was conscious of astonishment, an unsteady, wide-eyed comprehension: *This* was the reality. Earlier, they must have established over him an instantaneous and complete rapport. Now, they had to reach at him from the outside. His situation was showing continuous improvement. The spider creatures that had seemed so supreme were being deflated every instant. Four hundred ships had become one. A seemingly super-human mind control was now reduced to reachable size. He had no doubt that their threat to destroy him was on a physical level. What they meant was that they would use energy beams against him.

It was a far cry from their irresistible domination of his entire nervous system, but it was as dangerous as ever. He must play his game cautiously, and await an opportunity. He waited, and presently a thought was directed at him:

"It is true that you have successfully released yourself from our mental thrall, and have discovered that there is but one ship. However, we have further use of you, and therefore we must ask you to cooperate under the threat of immediate extermination if you refuse."

"Naturally," said Hedrock, an old and successful cooperator, "I'll do what is required unless it involves a near equivalent of extermination such as dismemberment."

"We have in mind," came the precise answer, *"a further sensory study of the Neelan twins. Since you were connected with the relationship when you were under our control, we can dispense with the twin on Earth, and work directly through you. There will be no pain, but you must yield yourself to the investigation."*

Hedrock protested, "I heard one of you say that Gil Neelan was dead. That was before I was put back on Earth. How can you work with a dead man?"

The reply was icy. *"Please allow us to handle the cell growth problems involved. Do you submit yourself?"*

Hedrock hesitated, "Are you going to let me live—afterwards?"

"Naturally not."

He had expected that answer, but it was a shock nonetheless. Hedrock countered, "I don't see how you can expect me to cooperate on such a basis."

"We will advise you of the moment of death. That will give you the emotional excitement you crave, and will thus conform to your requirements."

Hedrock said nothing for a moment. He was fascinated. These monsters thought they would be catering to human nervous requirements by telling him when he was due to die. That was as far as they had gotten in their investigation of man's emotional nature. It seemed incredible that anyone could miss the mark so completely. The intellectual approach of these creatures to life and death must be stoical in the extreme. Instead of trying to bite the hand that was reaching forth to destroy it, each individual spider probably examined all methods of escape and, finding none, accepted death without a struggle.

Hedrock said finally with a crisp ferocity, "You seem to have done pretty well, you and your kind. Here you are in a ship the size of a small moon. You obviously come from a mentally superior civilization; I'd like to see the planet that spawned you, its industries, its ordinary way of life. It should be interesting. Beyond doubt, your brand of logic has done well by you. Nature can pat herself on the back for a successful experiment in producing intelligence, but you've missed the point about man if you think that all I'm interested in is when I can expect to be killed."

"What more would you like to know?" There was interest in the questioning thought.

Hedrock said wearily, "All right, you win. I'd like to know when I can get something to eat."

"Food!" His questioner was excited. *"Did you hear that, —Xx-Y—(meaningless)?"*

"Most interesting," came another thought. *"At a critical moment the need for food is uppermost. It seems significant. Reassure him, and proceed with the experiment."*

Hedrock said, "You don't have to reassure me. What do you want me to do?"

"Yield."

"How?"

"Submit. Think of the dead body."

It was a relief to do that, and the picture grew remarkably sharp. He thought suddenly: Poor Gil, lying lifeless on a limitless sea of sand, his cells already collapsed from the ever rising pall of heat as the speedy planet drew ever nearer to one of its two parent suns. It was a strangely agonizing visualization for him, and yet, at the same time, thank God he was dead. The suffering was over. The mortal remains were beyond the pain of heat, beyond the ceaseless worry of the stinging sand, beyond thirst and hunger, beyond fear and unreasonable hope. Death had come to Gilbert Neelan as it must to all men. God bless him and keep him.

Hedrock deliberately stopped that intense emotional reaction. "Just a minute," he said, amazed. "I'm beginning to feel as if I *am* his brother."

"That," came a thought, *"is one of the astonishing characteristics of human beings. The easy way that one nervous system responds to the impulses from another. The sensory equipment involved has no parallel in the world of intelligence. But now, sit up and look around you."*

Hedrock studied his 'stat plates. He saw that there had been a change in the scene. The big ship, whose captive he was, had rolled upward; its immense bulk filled the forward and rear plates, and was visible also on the upper right and left panels. Where it had been before was a gulf of space, and deep in that gulf swam two white, yellow-tinged suns. They were tiny at first, little more than bright stars. But they grew. They grew. And far to the left another, tinier sun appeared. The two larger stars showed after a while six inches in diameter. They had seemed a foot apart; they separated farther. One remained small while the other drew nearer and took on more size. The second sun swung farther and farther to the left; his estimators showed it finally as about three billion miles away.

Further tests showed the angular diameter of both the nearer suns of the system to be larger than that of Sol, though only one was brighter. The third sun was a mere blur of light in the distance. It would have taken a long time for his inadequate instruments to compute its character. But the fact that it was there made Hedrock frown. He searched for, and presently found a red point in the distance, the fourth sun of that system. He was beginning to feel excited, when the alien mind directed its cold vibrations at him again.

"Yes, man, you are correct. These are the suns of the system you call Alpha Centauri. The two nearest are Alpha A and Alpha B. The third white sun is Alpha C, and the red point is, of course, the insignificant Proxima Centauri, known for centuries to be the nearest star to the solar system. These latter two do not concern us. What matters is that the dead twin is

127

*on a freak planet of this system. There is only one freak. It
is a planet which, by describing a figure 8, revolves in turn
around the Centauri suns Alpha A and Alpha B. It does this by
traveling at the unusual speed of three thousand miles a
second. In its eccentric orbit, it passes very close to each star,
much as a comet might. But unlike a comet it is forever unable
to break away. The gravitational fields of Alpha A and
Alpha B alternately whip it on its way. It is now approaching
ever nearer to Alpha A, the star almost directly ahead, and we
must work swiftly if we are to revive the dead body—"*

"If we are to *what*?" said Hedrock.

There was no answer, nor did he need one. He leaned
weakly back in his chair, and he thought, "Why, of course,
it's been obvious from the beginning. I took it for granted
they were going to try to rig up some sensory connection between a living and a dead body, but that was an assumption
based upon my conviction that a man who has been dead two
days is not only dead but decomposing."

He felt genuinely awed. For thousands of years he had been
striving to prolong the lives of living men to some approxima-
tion of the immortality that he had accidentally achieved.
Now, here were beings who could undoubtedly not only
solve that problem but could also resurrect the dead.

Curiously, the discovery dimmed his hope that he would be
able to survive in spite of their determination to kill him. He
had been trying to imagine some method of defeating them
based on their extremely logical approach to existence. But,
while that still seemed the only possible way out, it had become a remote chance, an opportunity to be planned for because the alternative was so final. Their scientific achievements
made the result extremely doubtful.

"You will now," said a thought impulse, *"submit to the
next phase."*

He lay under a light. Just where he was, or even where they
wanted him to think he was, he had no idea. His body rested
comfortably in what could have been a form-fitting coffin.
The comparison made a gruesome titillation along his nerves,
but he quieted that jumpiness. He lay steady, determined,
cold with his own intentions, and watched the light. It hung
in blackness above him or—the thought made a curious pattern—was he staring *down* at it? It didn't matter. There was
only the light, shining out of the darkness, shining, shining. It
was not, he noticed after a long while, a white light; and yet,
conversely, it seemed to have no definite color. Nor was it
bright, nor was it warm. His thought paused; he flinched. It
was the notion of heat that did it, that brought consciousness
of how cold it was. The light was icy.

128

The discovery was like a signal, like a cue. *"Emotion,"* said a spider's mind vibrations from afar, *"is a manifestation of energy. It acts instantaneously over any distance. The reason why the connection between the twins diminished in intensity, so far as their reception of it was concerned, was their mutual expectation that it would so diminish. This expectation was almost entirely unconscious. Their respective nervous systems naturally recognized the widening distance when one set out for Centaurus. Instinctively, they yielded their connection, though the emotional rapport between them remained as strong as ever. And now, since you have become a part of the relationship . . . accept the connection."*

It seemed instantaneous. He was lying, Hedrock saw, on a grassy bank beside a stream. The water gurgled and babbled over rocks. A gentle breeze blew into his face, and through the trees to his left a glorious sun was rearing above the horizon. All around him on the ground were boxes and packing cases, several machines, and four men lying quietly asleep. The nearest man was Gil Neelan. Hedrock controlled his mind again, thinking desperately, "Steady, you fool, it's only an image, a *thing* they've put into your brain. Gil is on sand, on a freak planet, headed into hell. This is a dream world, an Eden, Earth in its sweetest summertime."

Several seconds passed, and the body of Gil Neelan slept on with flushed face, breathing stentoriously, as if it couldn't get enough air into it, as if life was returning the hard way, and clinging with effort. A faint thought came into Hedrock's mind. "Water," it said. "Oh, God, water!"

He hadn't thought that. Literally Hedrock threw himself at the stream. Twice, his cupped hands trembled so violently that the precious water spilled onto the green grass. At last a measure of sanity came, and he searched one of the boxes and found a container. He kept letting the water trickle in and around Gil Neelan's mouth. Several times, the emaciated body contorted in dreadful coughing. But that too, was good —dead muscles jarring back to life. Hedrock, eyes glinting, persisted. He could feel Gil's slow heartbeat, could see all the mind pictures that pushed hesitantly into the brain that had scattered far. It was the sensory relation that, until now, had belonged exclusively to the brothers. Gil stirred in awareness.

"Why, Dan—" there was a vast amaze in Gil's thought— "you old devil! Where did you come from?"

"From Earth." Hedrock spoke aloud into the breeze that blew in his face. Later he would explain that he was not Dan.

The answer seemed all that Gil needed. He sighed, smiled, and turning over, withdrew mentally into a deep sleep. Hedrock began to prowl around the boxes, looking for dextrose tablets. He found a bottle of the quick-acting food, and slipped a tablet into Gil's mouth. It should, he thought, dissolve gradually. Satisfied that he had done all he could for the moment, he turned to the other men. He doled out water to each of the three in turn, and then dextrose tablets. He was straightening from the work when a spider-thought touched him, matter-of-fact in its steely overtones.

"*You see,*" it said, "*he did attend the others, too. The emotion involved is more than just an artificial extension of paired spermatozoa reacting sympathetically.*"

That was all there was, just that comment. But it stopped Hedrock in his tracks. It wasn't that he had forgotten the spiders. But the memory of them had been pressed into the background of his mind by the urgency of events. And now here was the reality again. He stared up into the blue sky, up at that glorious, yellow-white sun, and hated the spider folk. But that, he realized, was like savages of old shaking their fists and mouthing their maledictions at the evil demons who lurked in the heavens.

He grew calmer, and again fed his sick charges, this time a liquid made of highly digestible fruit juice concentrates dissolved in water. One of the men, a lean, handsome fellow, revived sufficiently to smile up at him in a puzzled fashion, but he asked no questions and Hedrock volunteered no information. When the patients were sleeping again, Hedrock climbed the tallest tree he could find, and studied his surroundings. But there were only trees and rolling hills and far, far away, almost lost in the mist of distance, a wider glint of water. What interested him more were patches of yellow color on a tree a quarter of a mile along the creek. He shinnied to the ground and walked with some excitement, following the stream bed. It must have been farther than he had estimated, for when he came back with a container full of fruit, the sun was past the zenith.

But the trek had done him good; he felt better, more alive; and he was thinking shrewdly: Gil and Kershaw—if one of these chaps was Kershaw—must have visited this planet. They must have tested the fruits they found, and as soon as they recovered sufficiently, they'd be able to tell him whether this yellow stuff was edible. There might even be a pocket analyser in one of the packing cases.

If there was, he couldn't find it. But he did uncover a number of instruments, including a recorder for communication disks, used in surveying and marking land sites. They probably had left a lot of those on their various points of landing. The sun lowered itself toward, well, the west. He'd call it that, Hedrock decided wryly. Late in the afternoon, the second sun came up in the east, tinier, a pale orb. For a while, then, it grew warmer, but cooled off when the larger sun sank behind the horizon, and "night" set in. It was like a dull day on Earth, with a ghost of a sun peering through heavy clouds, only the sky wasn't cloudy and there was none of the humidity and closeness of a dull day. Soft winds blew. The third sun came up, but its dim light seemed to add nothing. A few faint stars showed. The bright gloom began to get on Hedrock's nerves. He paced along the creek bank, and he thought finally: How long would this ... this sensory investigation continue? And why did they want to kill him?

He had not intended it as a direct question to his captors, but, surprisingly, he received an answer at once. It seemed to float at him out of the dim, cloudless sky, precise and supernally dispassionate:

"We are not quite what we seem," the spider-thought said. *"Our race is not, as you suggested, one of Nature's successes. In this ship is actually the remnant of our people. All of us here present are immortal, the winners in the struggle for supremacy and existence on our planet. Each and every one of us is supreme in some one field by virtue of having destroyed all competition. We intend to remain alive, our existence unsuspected by the several other races in the universe. Because of an accident that precipitated you into our midst, you must die. Is that clear?"*

Hedrock had no answer, for here at long last was a completely understandable logic. He was to be killed because he knew too much.

"It is our intention," said the cold mind at him, *"to make a final investigation of man's sensory equipment on the basis of what we have discovered through you, and then leave this portion of space forever. The investigation will take some time. You will please have patience until then. There will be no answers meanwhile to your petty appeals. Conduct yourself accordingly."*

That, too, was clear. Hedrock went back slowly to the camp. The lean, tired-looking man who had smiled at him earlier was sitting up.

"Hello," he said cheerfully. "My name is Kershaw. Derd Kershaw. Thanks for saving our lives."

"You're thanking me too soon," said Hedrock gruffly.

But the sound of the human voice brought a gathering excitement and, just like that, an idea. He worked, now that the hope had come, with an intense anxiety. He expected to be destroyed momentarily.

The job itself was simple enough. With Gil's energy gun, he cut trees into little round disks about an inch thick. The disks he kept feeding into the survey recording machine, which imprinted on the elements of each a message stating the position of himself and his companions, describing the spider folk and the threat they had made. For some of the disks, he set the recorder to various anti-gravity pressures, ten feet, twenty feet, fifty—up to five hundred—and watched them float up into the sky to the level their atoms had been adjusted for. They drifted in the vagrant currents of the air. Some just hung around and made him sweat with anger at the slowness with which they scattered. Others whisked out of sight with a satisfying rapidity. Some of them, Hedrock knew, would lodge on hillsides, some in trees, some would float for years, perhaps centuries, prey to every breeze that blew, and every hour that passed they would be more difficult to find, would take longer to search out. The spider folk were going to have a hell of a time preventing the knowledge of their presence from being spread abroad.

The precious days dragged by, and soon there was no doubt that enough time had gone by for the disks to scatter widely.

His patients were slow in recuperating. It was apparent that their bodies were not capable of absorbing properly the food he gave them, and that they needed medical care which was not available. Kershaw was the first to reach the convalescent stage where he wanted to know what had happened. Hedrock showed him the message on one of the disks, which, after three weeks, he was still sending out spasmodically. Kershaw read it and then lay back thoughtfully.

"So that's what we're up against," he said slowly. "What makes you think the disks will do any good?"

Hedrock said, "The spiders are logic hounds. They'll accept an accomplished fact. The problem is when will the process of distribution of the disks have reached a point where they'll instantly realize that they can't possibly ever find all of them? Every little while I think that surely I've done enough, and then I begin to wonder just how intricate will distribution have to be before they'll accept it as decisive. The reason they haven't bothered us so far is that they're near Earth studying man's emotional structure. At least that was their intention, and I was told they wouldn't talk to me for a while. My guess is they're too far away for their brand of telepathy."

"But what are they after?" Kershaw asked.

It was hard to explain what his own experiences with the spiders had taught him, but Hedrock made the attempt. He was careful to give no inkling of his activities on Earth. He

132

finished, "I can break their mental control at any time, so that their only threat against me is physical force."

Kershaw said, "How do you explain their ability to draw you back to the lifeboat in spite of your resistance?"

"I can only suggest that the nervous system is slow in setting patterns. I was back in the lifeboat before my method of opposition actually went into operation. When it did they recognized what was happening and threatened to destroy me unless I cooperated."

"Do you think they'll get anywhere in their attempt to understand human emotional nature?"

Hedrock shook his head. "For thousands of years men have been trying to gain ascendancy over their emotional impulses. The secret, of course, is not to eliminate emotion from life but to channel it where it is healthy and sane: sex, love, good will, enthusiasm, alertness, personality, and so on. These are apparently aspects of existence which are not within the possible experience of the spider beings. I don't see how they can ever understand, particularly because they have no method of distinguishing between a man who is willing to risk his life for a cause, and a man who takes a risk, for example, for gain. The inability to understand variations of human nature is a basic flaw, and forever bars them from real comprehension."

Kershaw was thoughtful. At last he said, "What are our chances of rescue?"

Hedrock said grimly, "Very good. I know it looks bad for us, but the spiders said they were definitely leaving this part of space. Why would they leave unless they have some reason to believe that soon great ships from Earth will be plying the Centauri traffic lanes? In my opinion the Empress will release the interstellar drive, and in these days of speedy manufacture they'll have hundreds of drives installed into spaceships within a few weeks. And the trip itself could be completed in little more than two days, if necessary."

"I think," said Kershaw quietly, "we'd better get busy. You've put a lot of those disks out, but a few thousand more can't hurt. You cut the trees and pile the disks. I'll feed them into the machine."

He stopped, and swayed in a curious fashion. His gaze flashed wildly up beyond Hedrock's head. Hedrock whirled and stared into the sky. He saw a ship. For a moment he thought it was the spider ship as seen from far away. And then the mottled hue of it in the sun, and the great letters on its bottom snatched his attention. The letters said:

The ship was not far away, but low down. It skimmed over them less than half a mile up; and turned slowly back toward them in response to their urgent telestat calls. It made the return run to the earth in just over forty-one hours of flight. Hedrock had taken the precaution of having Kershaw and Neelan identify him as Gil's brother, and so he landed without incident at Imperial City, and proceeded to one of his apartments.

A few minutes later he was connecting the apartment 'stat to one of his relay systems. By that roundabout fashion he called the Weapon Makers.

18

IT WAS PETER CADRON'S IMAGE THAT APPEARED ON THE PLATE. He was not looking at the screen at the moment of contact, but was talking with animation to someone who was out of Hedrock's line of vision. There was no sound, and Hedrock made no attempt to guess at what the former councilor was saying. He had time to wonder again how Cadron would receive him.

Nearly a month had passed since that night when he had been compelled to act against the Weapon Makers in self-defence. In spite of his personal admiration for the majority of the councilors, he had no regrets. Earth's immortal man must assume his life was worth saving. For better or for worse he was what he was, and all the world must put up with him so long as he could protect himself.

Cadron was turning toward the 'stat plate. He froze as he saw who it was, and then hurriedly he clicked on the sound control. "Hedrock," he said, "it's you!"

A smile of pleasure came into his face. His eyes lighted up. "Hedrock, where have you been? We've been trying to contact you by every means."

Hedrock said, "What is my status with the Weapon Makers?"

Cadron straightened a little. "I have been authorized," he said, "by the *retiring* council to apologize to you for our hysterical actions against you. We can only assume that we were all caught up in a kind of mob attitude based on tension. I am personally sorry for what happened."

"Thank you. That means definitely no plotting?"

"Our word of honor." He broke off. "Hedrock, listen, we've been sitting on tenterhooks waiting for you to call. The Empress, as you know, released the drive unconditionally on the morning following the attack."

Hedrock had learned that on the ship coming back to Earth, but all he said was, "Proceed."

Cadron was excited. "We have received from her a most remarkable offer. Recognition for the Shops and a share in the government. It's a surrender of the first order."

Hedrock said, "You're refusing, of course."

"Eh?" Cadron's image stared.

Hedrock went on firmly, "You don't really mean that the Council considered accepting. You must realize there can never be a meeting ground between two such diametrically opposed forces."

"But," protested Cadron, "that's one of the things you suggested yourself as a reason for your going to the palace."

Hedrock said steadily, "That was a blind. During this crisis of civilization we *had* to have somebody in both the Shops and the palace. Wait!"

He went on in a ringing voice before the other could interrupt, "Cadron, the Weapon Shops constitute a permanent opposition. The trouble with the opposition of the old days was that they were always scheming for power; all too frequently their criticism was dishonest, their intentions evil; they *lusted* for control. The Weapon Shops never must allow such emotions to be aroused in their followers. Let the Empress rebuild her own chaos. I do not say she is responsible for the corrupt state of the empire, but the time has come for her to attempt a vigorous house-cleaning. Throughout, the Weapon Makers will remain aloof, interested, but maintaining their great standards for the relief *throughout the galaxy* of those who must defend themselves from oppression. The gunmakers will continue to sell their guns and stay out of politics."

Cadron said slowly, "You want us then to—"

"Go about the routine of your normal business; nothing more nor less. And now, Cadron—" Hedrock smiled. "Cadron, I have enjoyed knowing you personally. Pass on my felicitations to the retiring council. I intend to present myself at the palace one hour from now; and none of you will hear from me again. Goodbye to all of you, and good luck."

He shut off the 'stat with a jerky movement and sat there conscious of that old, old pain of his. Once more he was withdrawing himself. He forced the great loneliness out of his soul at last and put his carplane down on the palace exactly on the hour. He had already called Innelda, and he was admitted at once to her apartment.

He watched her from half-closed eyes, as they talked. She sat stiffly beside him, a tall, graceful, long-faced woman whose green eyes hid her thoughts. They sat under a palm tree in the garden that was the reception room of the thirty-fourth floor. Soft breezes blew against them; the shaded lights shed a gentle glow over the quiet scene. Twice, he kissed her, conscious that her diffidence had an inner meaning that he must bring into the open. She took the kisses with all the passivity of a slave woman.

Hedrock drew back. "Innelda, what's the matter?" She was silent; and he pressed on, "The first thing I find, when I come back, is that Prince del Curtin, who has been almost literally your right hand, has been banished from the palace. Why?"

The words seemed to rouse her out of some depth. She said with a shadow of fire in her tone, "My cousin has had the temerity to criticize and oppose a project of mine. I will not be badgered even by those I love."

Hedrock said, "Badgered you, did he? That doesn't sound like the Prince."

Silence. Hedrock stared at her slantwise, then said in a persistent tone, "You practically gave up the interstellar drive for me, and yet now that you have me, I can't feel that it means anything."

During the long silence that followed, he had his first thought of what all this rigidity might be. Was it possible that she knew the truth about him? Before he could speak, her low voice came, "Perhaps all I really need to say, Robert, is that there will be an Isher heir, an *Isher* heir."

The child part of the revelation hardly touched him. She knew. That was what counted. Hedrock sighed finally. "I forgot. You caught Gonish, didn't you?"

"Yes, I caught him; and he didn't need very much more information than he had. A few words; and the intuition was complete."

He said at last, "What are you going to do?"

Her answer came, remote-toned, "A woman cannot love an immortal man. The relation would destroy her soul and her mind." She went on, almost as if speaking to herself, "I realize now I never did love you. You fascinated me, and perhaps repelled me a little, too. I'm proud, though, that I selected you without knowing. It shows the enormous instinctive vitality of our line. Robert!"

"Yes?"

"Those other empresses—what was your life like with them?"

136

Hedrock shook his head. "I won't tell you. I want you to make up your mind without even thinking of them."

She laughed in a brittle tone. "You think I'm jealous. I'm not ... not that at all." She added in a disjointed manner, "Henceforth, I'm a family woman who intends to have the respect as well as the affection of her child. An Isher Empress can do no other. But I won't press you." Her eyes darkened. She said with sudden heaviness, "I'll have to think it over. Leave me now, will you?"

She held out her hand. It felt limp under the pressure of his lips, and Hedrock went frowning to his apartment. Sitting there alone, he remembered Gonish. He put a call through the Weapon Makers exchange, and asked the No-man to come to the palace. An hour later, the two men sat facing each other. "I realize," Gonish said, "that I am to receive no explanations."

"Later," said Hedrock; then, "What are *you* going to do? Or rather, what have you done?"

"Nothing."

"You mean—"

"Nothing. You see, I understand just what the knowledge would do to the average and even the higher-type human being. I shall never say a word, not to the Council, not to anyone."

Hedrock was relieved. He knew this man, his enormous integrity. No fear was behind that promise, simply a stark honesty of outlook that would never be more than equalled. He saw that Gonish's eyes were studying him. The No-man said, "With my training, I would have quite naturally known better than to make a test of the effect of immortality on others. But you made it, didn't you? Where was it? When?"

Hedrock swallowed hard. The memory was like fire. "It was on Venus," he said in a flat voice, "during the early days of interplanetary travel. I set up an isolated colony of scientists, told them the truth, and set them to work to help me discover the secret of my immortality. It was horrible, oh—" His voice thickened in distress. "They couldn't stand watching my perpetual youth as they grew old. Never again."

He shuddered; and the No-man said quickly, "What about your wife?"

Hedrock was silent for a long minute. He said then, slowly, "The Isher empresses in the past have always been proud of their relation to the immortal man. For the sake of the children, they put up with me. I can say no more."

His frown deepened. "I've sometimes thought I should marry oftener. The immortal strain might, just might, repeat

137

that way. This is only my thirteenth marriage. Somehow, I didn't have the heart even though—" he looked up—"I've developed a perfect method of aging my appearance, enough to have a psychological effect on those who actually know the truth."

There was a look on Gonish's face that narrowed Hedrock's eyes. He said quickly, "What's the matter?"

The No-man said, "She loves you, I think; and that makes it very bad. You see, she can't have any children."

Hedrock rose up out of his chair, took a step forward as if he intended the No-man bodily harm. "Are you in earnest? Why she told me—"

Gonish was bleak. "We of the Weapon Shops have studied the Empress from childhood. Her file, of course, is accessible only to the three No-men and to the members of the Council. There is no doubt of it."

The No-man's gaze fixed Hedrock sharply. "I know this wrecks your plans, but don't take it so hard. Prince del Curtin is next in line and will carry on, rather strongly, I think. There'll be another Empress along in a few generations, and you can marry her."

Hedrock ceased his pacing. "Don't be so damned callous," he said. "I'm not thinking of myself. It's these Isher women. The trait hasn't shown clearly in Innelda, but it's there. She won't give up that child; and that's what I'm worrying about." He swung directly toward the No-man again. "Are you absolutely sure? Don't play with me, Gonish."

The No-man said steadily, "Hedrock, I'm not playing. The Empress Isher is going to die in childbirth and—" He stopped; his eyes fixed on a point beyond Hedrock.

Hedrock turned slowly, and faced the woman who stood there. The woman said in a cold voice, "Captain Hedrock, you will take your friend, Mr. Gonish, and depart from the palace within the hour, not to return until—"

She stopped and stood for a moment like a figure of stone. She finished with a rush, "Never," she said thickly. "Never come back. I couldn't stand it. Goodbye."

"Wait!" Hedrock cried piercingly, "Innelda, you mustn't have that child."

He was talking to a closed door.

19

IT WAS DEL CURTIN WHO GOT HEDROCK INTO THE PALACE ON the final day. "We've got to," the prince had whispered, "get somebody near her. She must listen to reason. My friends are going to advise that new doctor of hers, Telinger, that you're in. Just stick to your rooms until you're called."

Waiting was dreary. Hedrock paced the thickly carpeted floor, thinking of the months since he had been banished from the palace. Actually, it was the last few days that had been worst. The whisper had spread abroad. Hedrock heard it far and wide. It didn't come over the telestats. No official word was given out; just how it became known definitely was impossible to say. He had heard it sitting in the restaurants he sometimes frequented. He heard it walking along quiet streets. It drifted on thin breezes, and rose in briefly heard voices above the clamor of conversations on carplanes. It had not been evil in intent or in actuality. It was simply, there was going to be an Isher heir *any day*, and the excited world of Isher was waiting for the announcement. They didn't know it, but the day was now. The crisis came at ten o'clock at night. A message from Dr. Telinger brought Hedrock out of the study and up into the Imperial apartments.

Telinger, Hedrock found, was a middle-aged man with a thin face, which was wrinkled in dismay as he greeted his visitor. Doctor Telinger, Hedrock knew, was guilty of nothing but weakness. He had been dragooned into the Imperial service as a replacement for Doctor Snow, who had been summarily dismissed after being court physician for thirty years. Hedrock could still remember one day at the dinner table when Innelda had inveighed against Dr. Snow, calling him "an out-dated practitioner who's still palming himself off as a doctor on the strength of having delivered me into the world." There was no doubt that old Dr. Snow had told her the exact situation; and Innelda hadn't liked it. And there was also no doubt, Hedrock realized as he listened to Dr. Telinger, that the new doctor had never been granted the privilege of a too thorough examination. She had picked well. He looked the kind of man who would be too awed to override the resistance of his Imperial patient.

"I've just discovered the truth," he almost babbled at Hedrock. "She's under antipain, but I've left a communication gap. Prince Hedrock, you must persuade her. It's the baby or she, and her conviction that she will live is utterly unfounded. She has threatened me," he finished whitely, "with death if the baby does not survive."

Hedrock said, "Let me talk to her."

She lay in the bed, calm and still. There was no color in her cheeks, and the rise and fall of her chest was so infinitesimal that she seemed already dead. Hedrock was conscious of relief when the doctor placed the communicator mask gently over that quiet yet intense face. Poor tyrant, he thought, poor, wretched, unhappy tyrant, caught up by inner forces too great for her to command or think through.

He picked up his end of the communicator. "Innelda," he said tenderly.

"It's—you—Robert." The answer was slow in coming and yet fierce. "I told—them—not—to—let—you—come."

"Your friends love you. They want to keep you."

"They—hate—me. They think—I'm—a fool. But I shall show them. I *will* myself to live, but the child must live."

"Prince del Curtin has married a lovely and wonderful woman. They will have beautiful children, worthy of the succession."

"No child but mine—and yours—will rule in Isher's name. Don't you see, it is the direct line that matters. There has never been a break. There will not be now. Don't you see?"

Hedrock stood sad. He saw even more clearly than she did. In the old days when, under various aliases, he had persuaded Isher emperors to marry women to whom family was vitally important, it had not seemed possible that the trait could ever become too strong. Here was proof that it could be tragic. And what this unhappy woman did not realize was that the reference to her "line" was only a rationalization. She wanted a child of her own. That was the simple reality.

"Robert—will you stay—and hold my hand?"

He stayed, and watched the life force ebb away. Waited till death lay heavily on the chilling body, and the baby was a thing whose raucous yowling made him angry.

Half a light year distant, a hundred-mile-long ship got under way. Inside it, thoughts vibrated from mind to mind:

"*. . . The second general examination is almost as futile as the first in its basic results. We know some of the laws—but why did this ruler who possessed a world give her life for her child when in actuality she shrank from personal death? Her reasons that she personally must carry on her line are logically inadequate. It is only a matter of slight atomic rearrangement. Many men and women are alive who could carry forward her tribal progression.*

"It remains but to bring her back to life, and make a record of the emotional reactions of those around her to her resuscitation.

"...X-x??—has investigated the appearance of our former prisoner Hedrock at the palace, and it appears that he nullified by an ingenious method the logic that required his destruction. Accordingly, we can leave the galaxy within one ... period.

"This much we have learned. Here is the race that shall rule the sevagram."

NEL BESTSELLERS

Science Fiction

F.1233	THE OCTOBER COUNTRY	Ray Bradbury	3/6
F.1234	THE SMALL ASSASSIN	Ray Bradbury	3/6
F.2658	GLORY ROAD	Robert Heinlein	7/6
F.2659	STRANGER IN A STRANGE LAND	Robert Heinlein	10/6
F.2754	DUNE	Frank Herbert	12/-
F.2386	PODKAYNE OF MARS	Robert Heinlein	6/-
F.2449	THE MOON IS A HARSH MISTRESS	Robert Heinlein	8/-

War

F.2423	STRIKE FROM THE SKY—THE BATTLE OF BRITAIN STORY	Alexander McKee	6/-
F.1686	EASTERN APPROACHES	Fitzroy Maclean	7/6
F.2645	THE LONGEST DAY	Cornelius Ryan	5/-
F.2146	THE LAST BATTLE (illustrated)	Cornelius Ryan	12/6
F.2527	A SOLDIER MUST HANG	J. D. Potter	5/-
F.2471	THE STEEL COCOON	Bentz Plagemann	5/-
F.2494	P.Q.17—CONVOY TO HELL	Lund Ludlam	5/-
F.1084	THE GUNS OF AUGUST—AUGUST 1914	Barbara W. Tuchman	5/-

Western

F.2134	AMBUSH	Luke Short	3/6
F.2135	CORONER CREEK	Luke Short	3/6
F.2142	THE ALAMO	Lon Tinkle	3/6
F.2063	THE SHADOW SHOOTER	W. C. Tuttle	3/6
F.2132	THE TROUBLE TRAILER	W. C. Tuttle	3/6
F.2133	MISSION RIVER JUSTICE	W. C. Tuttle	3/6
F.2180	SILVER BUCKSHOT	W. C. Tuttle	3/6

General

F.2420	THE SECOND SEX	Simone De Beauvoir	8/6
F.2117	NATURE OF THE SECOND SEX	Simone De Beauvoir	5/-
F.2234	SEX MANNERS FOR MEN	Robert Chartham	5/-
F.2531	SEX MANNERS FOR ADVANCED LOVERS	Robert Chartham	5/-
F.2060	SEX AND THE ADOLESCENT	Maxine Davis	5/-
F.2136	WOMEN	John Philip Lundin	5/-
F.2333	MISTRESSES	John Philip Lundin	5/-
F.2382	SECRET AND FORBIDDEN	Paul Tabori	8/6
U.2366	AN ABZ OF LOVE	Inge and Sten Hegeler	10/6
F.2374	SEX WITHOUT GUILT	Albert Ellis Ph.D.	8/6
F.2511	SEXUALIS '95	Jacques Sternberg	5/-

Mad

S.3702	A MAD LOOK AT OLD MOVIES	4/6
S.3523	BOILING MAD	4/6
S.3496	THE MAD ADVENTURES OF CAPTAIN KLUTZ	4/6
S.3158	THE QUESTIONABLE MAD	4/6
S.2385	FIGHTING MAD	4/6
S.3268	HOWLING MAD	4/6
S.3477	INDIGESTIBLE MAD	4/6

— — — — — — — — — — — — —

NEL P.O. BOX 11, FALMOUTH, CORNWALL

Please send cheque or postal order. Allow 9d. per book to cover postage and packing (Overseas 1/- per book).

Name...

Address ....

....

Title ....
(NOV.)